Alfie Fleet's Guide to the Universe

Alfie Fleet's Guide to the Universe

MARTIN HOWARD

illustrated by CHRIS MOULD

OXFORD
UNIVERSITY PRESS

OXFORD
UNIVERSITY PRESS

Great Clarendon Street, Oxford OX2 6DP

Oxford University Press is a department of the University of Oxford.
It furthers the University's objective of excellence in research, scholarship,
and education by publishing worldwide. Oxford is a registered trade mark of
Oxford University Press in the UK and in certain other countries

British Library Cataloguing in Publication Data
Data available

ISBN: 978-0-19-276752-3

1 3 5 7 9 10 8 6 4 2

Printed and bound by CPI Group (UK) Ltd, Croydon, CR0 4YY

Paper used in the production of this book is a natural,
recyclable product made from wood grown in sustainable forests.
The manufacturing process conforms to the environmental
regulations of the country of origin.

FOR MY
MUM AND DAD
– M.H.

CHAPTER ONE

NEW PLANET INFORMATION SHEET

DISCOVERING · · · WINSPAN

One of the most spectacular 'broken worlds' in the universe, Winspan was formed when two planets crashed into each other. The colossal cosmic prang almost destroyed it and was a major inconvenience for the small, frog-like things who lived there. By the time the dust had cleared a few million years later, Winspan had lost its frog-folk but gained a new look—like half a dog-chewed tennis ball. Now surrounded by bright rings and thirty-six new moons, the planet's people live in the bowl around an ocean at the bottom. Its odd shape is only one of Winspan's attractions though. The planet lost a lot of gravity in the crash, so anyone can fly here, just by strapping wings to their arms and flapping. Today, the planet is a reminder that the universe is full of surprises and—if you're a small frog-thing—a reminder to enjoy each day as if it's your last.

Alfie Fleet, a sandy-haired boy with awkward knees, stepped out from between the pillars of a stone circle onto a different world. No one immediately threatened to wind his intestines around a stick or dangle his head from their belt. Alfie liked that. Not being in grave peril from the moment he stepped out of a circle was—for him—a plus. He grinned and wrote 'No' on his clipboard by the words GRAVE PERIL. Shading his eyes from the sunshine, he took a look around at Winspan's ocean landscape surrounded by endlessly high cliffs hung with vertical forests, clouds, and slow waterfalls. Winspan, he thought, scored about four on a scale he had invented, which he liked to call the Fleet Unusuality Scale. The air tasted fresh, the grass beneath his feet was green, insects buzzed, trees were made of wood and leaves, a sandy beach ran down to a sparkly blue ocean. It was the type of planet that would get a good review in the travel guide Alfie was writing.

A girl wearing a leather flying helmet and goggles and with white feathered wings strapped to her arms skimmed across the grass out towards the sea, squealing 'Wheeeeee'. She had a beak attached to the front of her helmet, Alfie noticed. Which was weird, but Alfie had visited weirder planets. The last he'd visited, Xardox, had been named after a brand of toilet paper.

Alfie took an experimental step. In the planet's

low gravity it turned into a giant leap for boykind. He landed softly, muttering, 'Yep, it's a four all right.' Planets with an unusuality score of four made excellent holiday destinations. Worlds with a score of more than five were too weird, and got on your nerves after a while. Places with a rating of less than three were so normal people might as well stay on Earth.

He wrote '4' in the right place on his clipboard. Winspan was definitely going in the travel guide. First though, he needed to find a place for visitors to stay. Shading his eyes again, he saw the distant cliff was dotted with round wooden doors and balconies. It looked like the people of Winspan made their homes by burrowing into the rock. Hopefully, they also made hotels and small-but-comfy bed and breakfast places, too.

'Here we are then, eh Rupert,' boomed a voice behind him. 'Good old Winspan, eh? Last time I was here was before the old queen died. Ooh . . . 1896, I think it was. Queen . . . ah what was her name? Tubby woman. Face like a bag of wasps.'

Alfie looked back over his shoulder to see

Professor Pewsley Bowell-Mouvemont walk
out from between the pillars of the stone circle.
A monstrous moustache clung to his upper lip like
two squirrels were sleeping up his nose. As usual,
the old man wore a long, dark green coat over a pink
frilly shirt. He creaked whenever he moved because
he was wearing a ladies' corset beneath his suit. He
said it was because he had a bad back though no-
one really believed him. The corset was decorated
with pretty bows and didn't look very medical.

'You mean Queen Victoria,' replied Alfie. 'And my name's *Alfie*, remember? I thought we were done with the "Rupert" nonsense.'

'Yes, that's her,' replied the Professor. 'Queen Viennetta. Queen Bag-of-Wasps-Face we used to call her whenever she popped down to the Unusual Cartography Club. Happy times, Rupert. Happy times.'

'*Alfie*,' repeated Alfie.

'Where?' said the Professor, looking around. Catching himself, he slapped his own face. 'Ah yes, *you're* Alfie,' he said. 'I don't know why you told me your name was Rupert in the first place. Having fun at an old man's expense, eh, you scamp? Young people today. Tsk. Mind you, Rupert, when I was a lad, just starting out at the UCC, we used to play some jokes, I can tell you. Once—you'll laugh at this—I broke into old Doctor Frobisher's sock drawer. Well, I'd stolen some salami from the kitchen you see, and . . .'

Alfie sighed. He wasn't the sort of boy who liked to interrupt, but a stroll down memory lane for the Professor could easily turn into a three-week hiking holiday. 'I *didn't* tell you my name was Rupert,' he interrupted. '*You* started it. Anyway, let's get on shall we? We've got a lot to do.'

'Of course, of course. Lots to do. Places to go, people to see. Busy, busy, busy. No rest for the . . . ah . . . early worm,' huffed the Professor. 'Umm, *what* do we have to do, exactly?'

Alfie shouldered his rucksack, and set out across the grass in long leaps. 'Well, first we have to find out if there's somewhere on Winspan where visitors can stay,' he called back over his shoulder. Checking his clipboard, he continued, 'Then we've got another planet to look at. Bewayre, it's called. The Nomefolk of Nomefolch asked us to buy them a new wheelbarrow, too. I thought we'd throw in a spade. They're *such* nice people. After that we need to make sure the Mystical Serpent of Nerwong Nerwong Plinky-Plonk is a *real* serpent and not a sock with buttons sewn on for eyes. There's a sky galleon to hire on Planet Scallion, and we *still* haven't got a group discount from Twerpz Tubeworms. We're seeing the Gloomy Emperor of Ominoss Murkwerld later, too. He's worried about packed lunches and . . .'

Let's take a moment while Alfie goes through his to-do list, shall we? Some readers might have dived straight into Book Two, skipping Book One altogether. Such readers might be thinking: 'What the heck is going on here? Who's this Alfie Fleet? What's he doing on planet Winspan? Why does the Mystical Serpent of Nerwong Nerwong Plinky-Plonk look like a sock with buttons stitched on?'

To those readers, we say a big welcome. Pull up a bookmark and make yourself comfy. For the full lowdown on what's going on you may wish to read Book One and come back later. It's available in all good bookshops and was described as 'a book with words in' by Jarvis O'Toole, author of *Grimly Gitfinger: The Nightmare Thief*, and 'the best book ever written where a dragon farts itself to death' in the review section of *City News*. It's got some snazzy artwork, too, so it's well worth a look-see. Still here? Well, all you *really* need to know is that in Book One, Alfie answered a job advert in a newspaper and knocked on the door of a falling-down house— Number Four, Wigless Square—the headquarters of an ancient intergalactic map-making society called the Unusual Cartography Club. In a cavern beneath the house he discovered a stone circle with the power to send travellers anywhere in the universe. As often happens, one thing led to another and after a bunch of adventures Alfie ended up as Vice-President of a new holiday company called the Unusual Travel Agency.

It's now two months later. Number Four, Wigless Square has been fixed up and Alfie and Professor Bowell-Mouvemont are almost ready to open the UTA's doors to the first intergalactic tourists. Before that happens they're checking out a few more worlds that might make good holiday destinations, and tidying up a few details.

Got it?

Marvellous, then let's get on with the story.

As we left Alfie and the Professor, they were leaping across the landscape of Winspan: a bouncing walk that brought them to the base of a cliff and a burrow with a golden birdcage hanging over its round, wooden door. Tables outside were packed with Winspanish folk, drinking from foaming mugs in the sunshine. Their strap-on wings were stored in racks, while waiters carried trays from a bar area inside. It looked very much like an inn, and was—therefore—*exactly* the sort of place Alfie and the Professor were looking for. It also looked peaceful and serene. Alfie nodded to himself and made a tick on his clipboard by the words PEACEFUL & SERENE.

Winspan seemed very promising indeed.

A few customers looked up as Alfie and the Professor approached. Like the girl Alfie had seen earlier, they wore flying helmets with different beaks attached at the forehead. A woman with a tray floated down to stop in front of them. Her helmet had a large duck beak. 'Tweet chirrup tweet tweet caw bok bok bikirk,' she said.

'Oh right, just a sec,' Alfie murmured. His fingers spun the handle on a small gramophone around his neck. A device invented by UCC President Madelaine Tusk in 1787, it translated every language in the universe. 'Sorry, say again,' said Alfie. The gadget around his neck sucked up the words and spat them from its trumpet attachment in perfect Winspanish.

'I said, welcome to *The Golden Cage*, my chicks.

I'm the innkeeper here,' the woman repeated. 'Debbi Puddlebeak of the Mottled Duck Clan.'

'Why ain't they got no wings?' shouted a man at the table behind her. He had a face full of freckles and cheerful red hair beneath a battered helmet decorated with a dinky beak. 'How're they supposed to get around if they ain't got no wings?'

'Shut your beak Stimpy Burntfeather,' said Debbi, 'I'm chirping, all right? Sorry, chicks, don't mind Stimpy. He's a Pigeon, and you know what Pigeons are like. Droppings for brains the lot of 'em.'

'Umm, yes, I remember now. You're all bird-people here on Winspan. Very interesting,' said the Professor. 'There are, of course, many bird-based societies around the universe. The Ostrich People on Planet Wungarr, for example, have extremely beady eyes, and the Chickenfolk of Tallon 6 . . .'

'We are visitors from planet Earth,' Alfie interrupted before the Professor could get properly started on his bird-folk lecture. 'We come in peace and so on and whatnot.'

'Planet what?' said Stimpy Burntfeather. 'What's he twittering about?'

'Planet *Earth*, Stimpy,' said Debbi Puddlebeak. 'Coo. Pluck me bald, they're only clucking *aliens* from another clucking planet.'

'Well that can't be right,' Stimpy replied. 'Where's their pointy heads? Where's their feelers? Where's their clucking space ship?'

'I have actually got quite a pointy head if you look closely,' the Professor chipped in, parting his hair. 'Look, it's like a church steeple . . .'

'We're not aliens,' said Alfie, trying to sound patient. He'd had to go through the same explanation many times while visiting different planets. 'We're human like you. We came through that stone circle over there. It works as a doorway between planets.'

'So you've travelled across space have you?' said Debbi Puddlebeak. 'Must be thirsty then. Can I get you some drinks? On the house for spacepersons.'

'That's very kind,' said Alfie. 'But we just have a few questions . . .'

'I still don't get it. How come you're human, if you comes from another planet?' shouted Stimpy. 'Aliens are supposed to be all funny-looking. Grey and squishy with big eyes and long, proddy fingers.

I've seen pictures.'

Alfie sighed. 'A long time ago humans travelled the universe . . .' he began, then thought better of getting bogged down in the story of how humans had once walked between worlds before forgetting the power of stone circles. 'Look it's a long story. My name's Alfie Fleet. Professor Bowell-Mouvemont and I . . .'

'Alfie Fleet's a funny name,' Stimpy chuckled.

'We're from a company called the Unusual Travel Agency and we're looking for a comfortable inn where visitors from Earth could stay,' Alfie continued. 'Are you interested, Ms Puddlebeak? It would mean extra business for you. Earth people will love flying, and I'm sure Winspan has a lot more to offer. We could bring the first tour group in a few weeks.' Digging around in his rucksack he handed Debbi Puddlebeak a copy of the UTA brochure, featuring questing holidays on Outlandish, spa breaks on the beach world of Blysss and much, much more.

Debbi flicked through the pages. 'It's all in alien writing,' she complained.

'You get the idea though,' Alfie replied. 'The Unusual Travel Agency offers holidays on the best planets in the universe, and yours is a beauty. People from Earth will come for the great Winspan experience. We'll also need to hire some local guides to show visitors places of interest, and flying instructors. We'll pay, obviously.'

'Coo, well my ducks, you Earth folk seem chirpy enough and if you're paying then I've got rooms. Stimpy here may be a dropping-brained Pigeon but he'll teach people to fly, won't you Stimpy?'

Stimpy nodded. 'Winspan flying champ six years in a row, me,' he said, proudly. 'Plus my sister's got a wing shop. Best wings on the planet.'

'There you go then,' said Debbi Puddlebeak, smiling at Alfie and the Professor. 'All sorted. Are you sure I can't get you chickies a drink?'

Alfie looked around. It was a beautiful day on Winspan and the view from *The Golden Cage*'s garden was fantastic. Above him, hundreds of fliers spread their wings, diving out from cliff-face cities and swooping over the glittering bowl ocean. He looked at the Professor, who nodded.

'Brilliant,' said Alfie turning and taking out his notebook. 'We do need to take a few more details so I'm sure we could squeeze in a drink.'

NEW PLANET INFORMATION SHEET

NAME OF PLANET: Winspan

NAME OF INSPECTOR: Alfie Fleet (Vice-President)

FLEET UNUSUALITY RATING: 4

TIME: 6x Earth Standard

WEATHER: Warm, single sun; occasional rain (water)

PRETTINESS LEVEL: 9; excellent for cliff fans; spectacular nights with 36 moons and beautiful sky rings.

GRAVE PERIL: No.

PEACEFUL & SERENE: √

INHABITANTS: Human, bird-based, friendly, ruled by the Dove Clan.

MAJOR TOURIST ATTRACTIONS: FLYING! Jewelled Nest of King Hoosa Prettyboy X (ruined); Vertical city of Sq'awk (shopping); The Crumbton Pecking Museum

NUMBER OF CIRCLES: 1 (known)

OVERALL TOURIST RATING: 8.5

CHAPTER TWO

ZERO-STAR REVIEW

DISCOVERING . . . BEWAYRE

Bewayre is a paradise for anyone with an interest in snot or starving to death. Anyone else should avoid it at all costs.

Alfie stepped out from between the stones of a circle onto a world a little over six billion light years from Winspan and immediately wished he hadn't. The happy-to-visit-a-new-planet grin dropped off his face and hit the ground with a clang. Dizzy, he took a

step to steady himself. Once again, the gravity was different from Earth's. On Bewayre it felt like he was walking through wet cake.

The planet was spinning fast, as if trying to throw him off. Above his head a giant red sun whipped across a sky of sulky clouds. Its cold, crimson light cast demonic shadows over a rocky landscape dotted with skulls. From somewhere came an endless depressing groan, like granddad on the toilet after a super-hot curry. The air smelled a lot like that, too. It put Alfie right off the sandwich he was holding. Tucking it in a pocket, he made a large zero on his clipboard by the words PRETTINESS LEVEL.

'Oh, I say,' puffed the Professor, strolling out of the circle behind him. 'I can't see this place being a hit with holidaymakers. It's ghastly. Smelly, too. Umm . . . why the heck did we come here?'

'It was your idea,' Alfie reminded the Professor. 'You found the coordinates down the back of the library sofa and said you wanted a look-see because no one had explored it before. There's no map in *The Cosmic Atlas*.'

'Did I say that?' The Professor sounded surprised. 'Oh yes, I did say that, didn't I? Ah, well, I *do* love an unexplored world. Nothing gets the blood whizzing like making a new map, eh? Measuring things is the best part. You simply *cannot* beat the thrill of measurement. As a boy I used to measure things all the time, you know. The kitchen table, Aunt Lucy's nostrils, cheese . . . Oh, those were exciting times, young Rupert.'

'Still, you can see why no one ever bothered measuring *this* place,' said Alfie wrinkling his nose. The stink was getting worse.

'Hmm, it *is* a miserable planet,' the Professor replied. Pointing, he continued. 'Some poor beggars live here though. I wonder what they do for fun?'

Alfie's eyes followed the Professor's finger. In the distance he saw a few wonky huts. They looked like they'd been thrown together from bones and scraps of skin. Thick smoke boiled from bent chimneys. Under the heavy gravity a sludgy gloop of it spread out across the ground, like sinister gravy.

Glancing at his pocket watch, which—like the Universal Translator—had been designed by Madelaine Tusk, the Professor squealed 'Cripes!' The hands were whirling around the face at an alarming speed. 'Time seems to be moving about twenty-five times faster back home, too,' he croaked. 'In the past minute half an hour of Earth time has passed. I think we can safely say that we won't be bringing tourists to Bewayre, eh Rupert?'

Let's take another moment there. Readers returning from Book One may remember that time moves at different speeds at different places in the universe. In some parts, it's all sort of bunched up, making time pass quite quickly. In *our* part, for instance, it's fairly sprightly, bouncing along at an average pace. In other parts of the universe time is all stretched out, crawling along like an elderly snail pushing a brick. Saying 'slow' and 'fast' is a bit confusing, of course, but time is like that: mostly baffling. A *lot* depends on where you're standing. The Unusual Travel Agency brochure featured many worlds where time moves more quickly so customers could squeeze in a two-week holiday during an Earth lunch break. It avoided slow-time worlds for the simple reason that no-one likes to get back from holiday to find their house is dust and the Earth is now ruled by Insect Overlords.

'Yeah,' Alfie agreed. 'Bewayre is grim. Let's go.'

Turning back towards the stone circle, Alfie found a spear pointed at his chest. Behind it two bloodshot eyes peered at him from a crusty face, which was exactly the right colour to make him think he was meeting a genuine—if crispy—little green man from outer space for the first time. 'We come in peace,' he said, because it's the sort of thing you're supposed to say to little green men from outer space.

The spear jabbed him in the chest.

Alfie groaned. Bewayre was one of *those* worlds then. Intergalactic travel was a lot of fun but it cheesed him off when people started poking him with spears before he'd even had a chance to say 'hello'.

'Interesting,' said the Professor, leaning forward to peer at the small green person. 'I suppose this answers my question about what they do for fun here. They smear bogeys on each other, apparently. I say, old chap, did you know you're absolutely *covered* in bogeys?'

'That's the kind of thing people usually know, Professor,' Alfie murmured. 'You don't get covered in bogeys and not notice.'

'Yes, you're probably right, Rupert,' the Professor agreed. 'Though there was a time on the planet Bumpadumtish when I . . .'

The bogey-covered Bewayrian interrupted the Professor. In a voice that sounded like its owner had swallowed a handful of pebbles, he said, 'Lak lak smak-a-lak-a-dribble lok doing wunge.' He then prodded Alfie again.

Moving the point of the spear to one side with a finger, Alfie wound the gramophone around his neck and said, loudly, 'If you don't mind, we're in a hurry.' As always, the device around his neck translated.

'Gimme,' the spear man croaked.

'Give you what?' said Alfie.

'Everything,' said the man poking Alfie with his spear. 'I King Bogeyface. You give clothes. Food. Everything.'

Alfie hesitated. He and the Professor were being mugged at spear point—and that annoyed him— but little King Bogeyface was skeleton-thin, and shivering in a few rags under the cold red sun. Plus, the planet's horrible smell had made him lose his appetite.

He handed over his sandwich.

King Bogeyface took a bite, then passed it over his shoulder. The crowd behind him tore it apart, small fragments of bread and cheese disappearing into their faces. 'Now clothes,' growled the king. 'Then we eat *you*. Plump and tasty. Yum yum. Taste like mum used to taste.'

Alfie rolled his eyes. Bewayre was shaping up to be at least a six on the Fleet Unusuality Scale, and was definitely not a suitable tourist destination. He made another cross on his clipboard.

'*Pff*,' said the Professor, 'If I had a penny for every time someone wanted to eat me I'd have thirty-six pence by now . . . Oww, he just poked me with his spear. Did you see that, Rupert? What in heck's name did you do that for, you bogey-crusted oaf!'

'Clothes. Then eating. Munchy munchy,' King Bogeyface repeated, poking the Professor again. 'You insult King Bogeyface. We eat you first.'

Alfie thought through his options. He couldn't help but feel sorry for the Bewayrians. After all, it wasn't their fault that they lived on a dried-up dog poo of a planet. On the other hand he didn't particularly want to be eaten. Time was whizzing past on Earth, too, and he and the Professor had a lot to do. There was only one thing for it. Digging a hand into his pocket, he said, 'Should I . . . you know . . . ?'

'I think you'll have to, young sprout,' said the

Professor. 'This chap is a bit of a pest.'

'It doesn't seem fair,' sighed Alfie. 'I mean, these people look like they've got enough problems.'

'Well, he *is* poking me with a spear,' said the Professor.

'Gimme,' repeated King Bogeyface, prodding Alfie with his spear this time. 'Gimme clothes *now*.'

'Do you mind, we're *trying* to have a conversation,' Alfie said. 'Oh well, I suppose there's nothing else for it.' Taking his hand from his pocket he tossed a small rock wrapped in paper back through the stone circle. 'I'm sorry for what is about to happen,' he told King Bogeyface. 'But you *are* being quite rude and I *did* say we were in a hurry.'

On the other side of the universe, Alfie's rock bounced out from between the pillars of the stone circle beneath Number Four, Wigless Square. The ancient headquarters of the Unusual Cartography Club had really smartened up its act since Book One ended. A LOT of dragon gold had been spent on it. Polished metal letters on the wall of the circle cavern spelled out **THE UNUSUAL TRAVEL AGENCY**. The jumbled piles of souvenirs from a thousand years of universal exploration were now displayed in glass cabinets. A sleek gift shop counter had been set up and stacks of ancient books had been moved to the library to make way for stacks of glossy UTA brochures. A seating area had been set up in a small departure lounge and a sound system put in for departure and arrival announcements. Framed posters hung on freshly painted white walls, showing the elf prince Hoodwink, who Alfie and the Professor had met on Outlandish. He had become an internationally-famous supermodel since moving to Earth. In one picture, Hoodwink grinned on a sunlounger, his hair beaded and a sweatfruit cocktail in his hand. In another, Hoodwink sat astride a tubeworm, expertly grasping its reins. In a third, Hoodwink busted moves on a dancefloor while the supernovas of the Volatile Sector exploded in the sky above.

A hand picked up the rock. Alfie's mum unwrapped the paper and peered at the word written on it in black felt tip: 'Help!'

'*Tsk*, they're in trouble again,' she said. 'Could you go fetch them, sweetie?'

A girl with long dreadlocks looked up from polishing an elderly moped called Betsy and pushed the headphones she was wearing off one ear. This was Alfie's closest friend: an orphaned girl named Hunter-Of-The-Vicious-Spiny-Dereko-Beast—or Derek for short. 'Eh?' she said. 'What was that, Mrs Alfie's mum?'

'Just "Mum" will do, honey. We've talked about this. I said, be a love and go save Alfie and the Professor from certain death again, would you.'

'That's the sixth time this week,' Derek grumped. 'And I'm busy.' She waved her polishing rag.

'I know, but what can you do?' Alfie's mum shrugged.

'Oh all *right*.' Replacing her headphones, Derek bunched her hands into fists, and walked into the stone circle.

Back on planet Bewayre King Bogeyface poked the Professor with his spear for the last time. 'Munch-munch *now*,' he growled.

At that exact moment Derek walked out of nowhere from between the pillars of the stone circle. Still listening to her favourite song by pop sensation

Jamie Fringe, which was called *Yeah Baby, Yeah*, she jumped between King Bogeyface and Alfie, giving the crusty Bewayrian king a wink. 'Hi,' she said, loudly. 'My name's Derek and I'll be your beater-upper today. Unless you'd like to take this once-in-a-lifetime opportunity to put the spear down and get lost.'

King Bogeyface did not take Derek up on her once-in-a-lifetime opportunity. Instead, he jabbed at her with it.

Alfie sucked in a breath. 'Ooo,' he muttered to the Professor. 'That was a mistake.'

'Mmm,' the Professor agreed, murmuring 'Ouch' to himself as Derek became a tornado of fists and dreadlocks.

'She has excellent footwork,' he continued a moment later, flicking a flying bogey from the shoulder of his jacket.

'Her fistwork's not bad either. I guess she *was* the Under-Sixteens Unnecessary Violence Champion on Outlandish . . . *Ooof*, that was nasty,' Alfie replied. His face screwed up in sympathy for King Bogeyface when Derek planted another punch.

With a grunt, the king dropped to the ground like a stunned owl.

The rest of the Bewayrians shuffled backwards, looking nervous as Derek snapped his spear across her knee, tossed the two halves over her shoulder and turned to face them. Crude weapons—mostly rocks and pointed sticks—clattered to the ground. 'We not with King Bogeyface,' squeaked a skinny man near the back.

'King who?' croaked another. 'I just out for a stroll. Never seen him before.'

Because he liked to practise his Outlandish, Alfie called 'P'turr spang churt t'ping spongecake, Derek. Spit spit dollop 'f'pask omelette.'

Derek glanced at Alfie. Slipping her headphones down she said, 'What?'

'P'turr spang churt t'ping spongecake, Derek. Spit spit dollop 'f'pask omelette,' Alfie repeated.

'Please fill your underwear with warm seaweed?' Derek had been learning English for two months and was *much* better at it than Alfie was at speaking Outlandish.

'Is that what I said?' Alfie replied, giving the

translator a shake. It needed another wind. 'I was *trying* to say, "Thanks Derek. You can leave them alone, it's time to go."'

'Warm seaweed in your underwear,' Derek repeated. 'That's what you said. Twonk.'

'It doesn't matter. Let's get out of here.' Unslinging his rucksack, Alfie rummaged inside, then tucked a colourful UTA brochure under King Bogeyface's unconscious head. Meeting the Professor's questioning look, he added, 'We *always* leave a brochure. Plus, he looks like he could use a relaxing sunshine break.'

The Professor stared down at the unconscious king of Bewayre. 'I suppose so,' he said. 'Though he looks quite relaxed already.' With a shrug, he walked between the stones and vanished.

'I've got bogeys all over me,' said Derek, peering down at herself.

'Sorry about that.'

Derek shrugged. 'It's all right. They're pretty. So, that's twenty-six times I've saved your life now.'

'I make it twenty-five.'

Slipping her headphones back on, Derek replied,

'Whatever. I can't hear you now.'

'Hey, wait . . .' Alfie said, but he was talking to thin air. Derek had already disappeared into the stone circle.

With a sigh, Alfie took a last look around Bewayre. On the horizon a huddled group of ragged people were leading a thin donkey through a cloud of dust towards the circle. Alfie felt sorry for them. The fight between Derek and King Bogeyface was about as much excitement as the planet had to offer, and they'd missed it. He shrugged and stepped between the great, grey stones of the circle. As always the universe opened up and swallowed him. But not before something odd happened. Above the granddad-on-the-toilet groan of Bewayre a voice echoed in his ears: a faint and distant voice that didn't need to be translated by Madelaine Tusk's gramophone gizmo. An English voice that said, 'Gadzooks. Our expedition is over. We're going home at last . . .'

CHAPTER THREE

PLANET OF THE NOMEFOLK

'Who said that?' said Alfie, looking from side to side as he stepped out into the stone circle cavern beneath Number Four, Wigless Square. Beneath the high, arched ceiling he blinked in the light of a hundred stylish spotlights that had cost a small fortune.

'Who said what?' Alfie's mum looked up from a shelf in the gift shop where she was stacking Hoodwink Haircare products under a sign that said 'Elf & Beauty'.

'Someone said "gadzooks".'

'Well it wasn't me,' said his mum. 'I've never

said "gadzooks" in my life. I might say "gadzooks" one day, but today is not that day.'

'Wasn't me, either' said Derek, pulling back her headphones. 'But I once kicked an enemy warrior in the gadzooks. He cried for days.' She returned to polishing Betsy, humming along to the chart-busting sounds of Jamie Fringe.

'Gadzooks, eh? It does sound like the sort of thing I *would* say,' said the Professor. 'It's a smashing word. Not as good as "shrimpkittens" but a fine word all the same. I don't think I *did* say it though, unless of course I was having one of my moments. I woke myself up last night shouting the word "hair", you know.'

'It didn't sound like your voice, Professor,' Alfie told him. He shrugged. 'Probably a glitch in the translator. Anyhoo, that's Bewayre crossed off the to-do list. Let's get on. Nomefolch next. Professor, do you want to spin the circle, or shall I?'

DISCOVERING . . . NOMEFOLCH

Everything is enormous on Nomefolch, where trees grow so tall it's possible to climb all the way into space. Only the planet's people are somewhat stubby, but what they lack in height they make up for in jolliness and bright red noses. Here, visitors will stay in cosy comfort inside giant, hollowed-out mushrooms, enjoying peaceful forest walks, strolls through attractive Nomefolch vegetable gardens, or fishing on giant lily pads. Every night the trees sparkle with lights and echo with music. Join in the fun by singing along to catchy Nomefolch hits like *Wheelbarrow 'Til I Die* and *She Was Only a Wheelbarrow Girl*.

An Earth hour later, Alfie and the Professor stood before the Nomefolchian Mayor, who was perched on the legendary Mushroom Throne, red boots kicking in excitement. His pointy red hat nodded, bell tinkling, as he looked his new wheelbarrow up and down. It was green with snazzy red handles. 'You bring a handsome gift,' he said. 'Built for speed a wheelbarrow like that. I bet it handles beautifully around corners.'

'The Unusual Travel Agency opens in less than a week,' Alfie told him. 'With your permission, we'll bring the first tourists from planet Earth soon after. And as you don't use money on Nomefolch they'll pay in . . .' Alfie opened his notebook and read his own notes. 'More gardening tools,' he finished.

'Splendid,' grinned the Mayor. 'We're looking forward to whatjamacallems . . . *tourists* . . . stimulating the local crummeny, like you said.'

'The local *economy*,' Alfie corrected. 'Wheelbarrow sales will rocket.'

The Mayor reddened. 'I should think NOT,' he squealed. 'A Nomefolchian's wheelbarrow is passed down through the generations. We'd sooner sell our grandmother's compost heap. But look you, we had a meeting and we've had some ideas to give visitors a real Nomefolch experience.' With a wave of his hand, he directed Alfie's attention to some freshly painted signs in the corner of the throne room.

PEOPLE OF EARTH!
GET THROWN OVER
THE BIG WATERFALL
IN A BARREL. ONLY
ONE TROWEL!

RUN AWAY FROM
OUR ANGRY
SCABBY GOAT.
SCABBY SCABBY
FUN FOR ALL THE
FAMILY!

ENTER OUR WEEKLY KNOBBLY
HEAD COMPETITION. HAS *YOUR*
HEAD GOT WHAT IT TAKES
TO BE A CHAMPION KNOBBLY
HEAD?

'We made some of them thingamajigs you told us about . . . *souvenirs* . . . too,' said the Mayor flapping his hand at a table covered with small statues of red-nosed Nomefolchians wearing pointy red hats and stripy leggings. Some were sitting on lily pads holding fishing rods, others were pushing wheelbarrows. 'We thought people might like to put them in their gardens when they get home.'

'I say, they look just like those *ridiculous* gnomes . . .' the Professor started.

'They look *great*,' Alfie interrupted quickly,

nudging the Professor. 'So, I think that's all we need for now, Mr Mayor. We look forward to sending the first tour group soon.'

'Where next?' asked the Professor as he and Alfie walked out into forest strung with fairy lights to the distant sound of Nomefolchians singing *Oh, Those Wheelbarrow Nights*.

'*The Happy Dragon* for a takeaway, I think,' said Alfie. 'It must be lunchtime on Earth and they pinched my sandwich on Bewayre. I'm starving.'

'How's Mr Hong?' Alfie asked while munching the last mouthful of sweet and sour chicken a little later. Mr Hong was the owner, cook, and waiter at Wigless Square's only restaurant.

'Miserable,' said his mum. 'We're his first customers this week.'

'Poor Mr Hong,' said Alfie. 'Hopefully he'll get more people coming in when we open.' Swallowing the last mouthful, he added, 'Finished, Professor? Nerwong Nerwong Plinky-Plonk next.'

'Take Derek with you this time,' said his mum. 'I don't want you to get eaten by a mystical serpent.'

'It's probably just a sock with buttons sewn on, Mum,' said Alfie. 'With one of the priests behind a curtain doing the voice. Last time we were there it told me I was going to change the universe. It's a big fake.'

'Whatever,' said his mum. 'I'll feel a lot happier if you take Derek.'

'Bango bango, f'uff bleep asparagus,' Derek muttered, in Outlandish. This won't be translated here because it contains unsuitable language.

'Aww, come on Derek, it'll be fun,' said Alfie, grinning at her. 'You might get to wrestle a sock puppet.'

Derek brightened up. 'Oh all right then,' she said, jumping to her feet.

'If I remember right, which happens from time to time, it's a mile or two from the circle to the Temple of the Mystical Serpent, so we'll take Betsy shall we?' said the Professor, strapping on a crash helmet. His corset creaked as he climbed onto the moped's saddle. 'Rupert, if you'd be kind enough to spin the circle and climb on board . . . Derek, old chap, you'll be running alongside as usual, I suppose?'

'Yeah.'

'Off we go then,' crowed the Professor. He stamped on Betsy's starter. Her engine puttered into life. 'Are you ready, Rupert? Toot toot.'

Alfie grinned and stepped up to put his hand on one of the stone pillars. The circle needed only the lightest of pushes to spin. Alfie checked the coordinates for the planet of Nerwong Nerwong Plinky-Plonk in *The Cosmic Atlas*, which lay open on a stand nearby. All he had to do was line stones up properly with a ring set into the floor and . . .

Alfie frowned. The circle was buzzing beneath his hand. 'Yikes', he muttered. 'Hey Professor,' he shouted over his shoulder. 'Something's happening to the circle. I think it's . . .'

He got no further. A stick appeared from between the stones, planted itself in his chest and shoved him.

Staggering backwards, Alfie stared as the stick was followed by a man's body. He was iron-faced and black-haired. A huge boil leaked yellow goo down his cheek into a pointy beard. Everything he wore was

ripped, battered, and covered in dust. Filthy tights
wrinkled down his legs. Peculiar puffy shorts made
it look like he'd put his legs through two deflated
beach balls. A sad looking ruff drooped around his
neck and a scruffy velvet cowpat of a hat sat atop
his head, its broken feather dangling.

The stranger waved a copy of the Unusual Travel
Agency's brochure in Alfie's face. '*GADZOOKS*,' he
roared. 'You horrible bunch of *traitors*.'

CHAPTER FOUR

UNWANTED ARRIVALS

Betsy's engine died. Jaws hanging open, Alfie, Derek, and the Professor watched as the man marched into the circle cavern, glaring around the room. Behind him, more people crowded through the circle like actors from a Shakespeare play, if Shakespeare had written a play about a bunch of people with *really* bad teeth. The first four to arrive had just enough left in their mouths to fill a matchbox. All of them— the people, not their teeth—wore the kind of clothes that had last been fashionable five hundred years ago, and which had looked deeply silly even then. The men's tights, especially, were a sharp reminder of why most men had given up wearing tights long,

long ago.

First through the circle was a small, rat-faced man with greasy hair and a pair of ancient spectacles perched on his nose. One of the lenses had fallen out, making one eye look much bigger than the other. He was leading a thin donkey on a rope, its back piled high with rusty pans, scrolls of parchment, and old-fashioned map-making equipment.

This answered the question of who had said 'gadzooks,' Alfie thought to himself. He had seen the donkey before: in the distance on Bewayre. He quickly did some calculations in his head. It was four hours since he, the Professor, and Derek had left that horrible planet, which meant about ten minutes had passed there. Time enough for the group of people he'd seen to reach the circle and find the brochure he had left. Now they were up close it was clear none of them was Bewayrian. For a start, none of them followed the Bewayrian fashion of sticking bogeys to their faces. That was a dead giveaway. And the iron-faced man spoke English, too, though he had a weird, old-fashioned accent.

They were obviously from Earth, but who they were and what they'd been doing on Bewayre was a mystery almost as deep as their fashion sense. Behind the rat-faced man was a woman wearing a lopsided, half-bald wig of tight red curls and a torn, hooped skirt so big that clowns, lion tamers, and trapeze artists could have put on a show beneath it.

A man with monkey-long arms thick with muscle stood beside her. The blank look on his face told Alfie he was the kind of person who had decided that thinking was too much fuss and bother. His tongue poked from the side of his graveyard mouth as if trying to escape the horrors within.

Last through was a boy about Alfie's age. It was difficult to tell because of the dirt clinging to his face, but Alfie guessed he might be the least hideous of the new arrivals. His full set of teeth and thick blond hair definitely gave him a head start on the rest of his companions.

When five people and a donkey stood in a ragged group before the stone circle the donkey lifted its tail and pooped: the horrible dribbly poop of a very unwell donkey. It immediately began soaking into the carpet.

Shocked, Alfie finally managed to speak, squeaking, 'Hey, that's an expensive carpet! I hope you're going to clean it up!'

'*Silence*, biscuit-faced villain!' bellowed the iron-faced stranger. 'I'll whip the skin off your backside, see if I don't.'

'Heh, my lord,' snickered rat-face. 'Whip the skin off his backside. Good one. That's *him* told. *He* won't need telling again, the scab-munching, ricket-kneed, snivelling little toad-fiddler.'

Derek cracked her knuckles. 'Nice of you all to drop by,' she said, quietly. 'I haven't had a fight in *hours*.'

Silence fell. Five heads turned. Five pairs of eyes stared at Derek.

The woman was the first to speak. Curling her lip, she squealed, 'Vile. The *foreign* girl looks like a Child of Skingrath from *Outlandish*. How utterly *ghastly*. It's such a *common* little planet.'

'Things here are worse than we thought,' growled the leader.

Derek growled. 'Right,' she hissed. 'I'm going to pull your face off and use it as a doormat.'

'Easy, Derek. I'll sort this out,' Alfie told his spitting friend. Turning back to the new group, he asked, coldly, 'Who are you? What do you want?'

Instead of answering, the oddly-dressed folk stared around at the cavern room.

'*Dreadful*,' sniffed bad-wig woman. 'We'll have to redecorate.'

'There's elves on the walls,' said rat-face man with a cackle. 'They've brought selfish, vicious, stinking, *elves* to Earth, my lord. That's a crime that is.'

'Prince Hoodwink isn't selfish . . .' Alfie checked himself. Hoodwink was, in fact, astonishingly selfish. 'I mean, he's not vicious . . . that is, he doesn't *stink*. He's quite finickety about personal hygiene, actually.'

'If I want you to speak, I'll *order* you to speak, you repulsive little bunty-waister,' roared the big man, glaring at Alfie. 'Keep your filthy pie box SHUT!'

'No, sir. You shut *your* pie box,' said the

Professor, striding forward. 'I don't know where you've slithered in from, but *I* am in charge here and . . .'

To Alfie's surprise, the stranger interrupted the Professor by laughing: a belly-shaking laugh with no humour in it at all. Flicking through the Unusual Travel Agency brochure he was holding, the man peered at the page that said 'Meet Our Tour Guides'. Looking up, he poked the Professor on the nose. 'Ah yes, you're the leader, aren't you? Professor *Pewsley* Bowell-Mouvemont,' he sneered. 'Author of *Around the Universe in a Corset*. President of the *Unusual Travel Agency*.'

Behind him, rat-face sniggered. '*Oooo*, lovely poking, my lord,' he said. 'That'll learn him. He'll not forget a poking like that in a hurry.'

From the corner of his eye, Alfie saw that the boy was staring at his feet, looking embarrassed.

'You *poked* me,' squeaked the Professor. 'Of all the cheek! I've had just about enough of you, sir. One moment, please.' He was already shrugging off his coat. 'Hold this, Rupert,' he said, handing it over. Rolling up the sleeves of his shirt, he put his fists up, ducking and dodging from side to side and punching the air, shouting, 'Come on then.'

'*Professor!* Stop that! What on Earth is going on?'

Now the arrivals' heads turned toward Alfie's mum.

'I believe it's a *woman*,' said bad-wig lady, looking her up and down rudely. 'Though how anyone could tell I have no idea.'

'She's wearing *trousers*,' said rat-face.

'*Disgusting*,' said the woman. 'You can see where her legs are.'

'If one more person says anything about my mum—*anything*—there will be trouble,' Alfie growled, his own hands clenching into fists.

'It's all right Alfie, leave this to me,' said his mum in the smooth but icy voice of a properly cheesed off mum. 'These people obviously have ways different from our own. Let's find out what they want. Then they can leave.'

'And who might *you* be?' asked the big man, staring at Alfie's mum.

'I run the gift shop here. Who are yo—'

'And what sort of beastly thing is a "gift shop"?'

'When we open, it will sell mugs and t-shirts and souvenirs to the tourists,' said Alfie's mum. 'I repeat: who are yo—'

The man lifted a finger to stop her. 'We will throw your mugs and rubbish out into the street,' he growled. 'There will be no "gift shop" at my Unusual Cartography Club.'

'You'll do no such thing, you . . . you . . . wait, *what* did you say?' The Professor blinked at the man. The colour drained from his face. 'Who *are* you?' he croaked.

'Ah, I see the old fool is beginning to understand,' said the big man, grinning a grin that dripped evil. 'My name is Sir Willikin Nanbiter, and I am President of the Unusual Cartography Club.'

CHAPTER FIVE

ONE PRESIDENT TOO MANY

The Professor goggled. His jaw sagged as if it had come away at the hinges. 'Sir Willikin Nanbiter,' he finally managed to gurgle. 'President of the Unusual Cartography Club from 1542 to 1546 when you left to lead a mapping expedition to . . . to . . .'

'Bewayre,' Willikin Nanbiter hissed. 'Yes. Our mission there is now complete. For sixteen years we have mapped every corner of that wretched planet. With only a length of string we measured it from Sir Willikin's Land in the far north to the Nanbiter Peninsula in the south. We have braved snot-crusted cannibals, eaten only leeches . . .'

'Umm . . . actually, leeches are quite good if you fry them up with . . .' The Professor started.

'Be SILENT, you mouldering heap of cabbage dung,' Nanbiter bellowed into his face.

The Professor took a step back.

'And *finally* we returned to the stone circle from where we started,' Nanbiter continued. 'Victorious! Our great map of Bewayre finished. We expected a welcome for heroes. Instead, we find this . . . this *outrage*.' Red-faced, Nanbiter once again waved the UTA brochure Alfie had left with King Bogeyface.

'Ah yes, our new brochure,' said the Professor. 'I expect you're wondering . . .'

Sir Willikin Nanbiter interrupted again. 'The date,' he hissed, smacking a fist onto the front cover. 'Almost five hundred years have passed since we set out on our noble expedition. And worse than that . . . much, *much* worse than that, the Unusual Cartography Club is no more. Gone. And in the place of our fine and secret map-making society what do we find? A company selling HOLIDAYS.' He screamed the last word.

The Professor took another step back, blinking. 'As you say, almost five hundred years have passed since you left, Sir Willikin. Umm . . . welcome home, I suppose. We've gotten off on the wrong side of the bed, eh? Laugh about it later, I'm sure.'

Nanbiter leaned forward. Pushing his face up against the Professor's, he bellowed, '*Laugh!* I don't see anything to *laugh* about you earwax-brained box of mouse farts. *Traitor*. Reveal the secrets of the Unusual Cartography Club, would you? Allow a foreigner from one of the lesser worlds to join our lovely society? Let common gutter-spankers use *our* stone circle to go on their *holidays?*'

Leaving spit all over the old man's face, he turned to Alfie and waved the brochure in his face again. 'And *you*, Alfie Fleet, a knock-kneed, scallywag *apprentice*. I see here that you *dare* to call yourself Vice-President of our glorious club?'

Alfie took a step backwards. 'It's not like anyone else wanted the job,' he said.

'That's *enough*,' yelled his mum. '*You* . . . Sir Wilbert or whatever your name is . . . get away from my son or so help me I'll . . .'

'You'll stay out of this, *gift shop* woman,' screeched Nanbiter. 'This is *my* house, and you'll speak when I tell you.'

'Bless my . . . ahh . . .' started the Professor, angrily. 'Oh, what's the word I'm looking for? You find them on the bottom of shoes.'

'Soul,' Alfie whispered.

'That's it. Sole, of course. I knew it was something to do with fish. Look here, Sir Willikin. I understand you've had a challenging expedition, and it must be a shock to find so much time has passed since you left. However, in this day and age *I* am the President around here and I ask you to remember your manners.'

'You'll ask for *nothing!*' shouted Nanbiter. Standing tall, he raised his hand and bellowed, 'All who vote for Sir Willikin Nanbiter to take back control of the Unusual Cartography Club, hands up now.'

Behind him, four hands were raised. The boy, Alfie noticed, was still staring at his feet, though he raised his hand slowly. 'Five votes for Sir Willikin,' Sir Willikin roared. 'Let's see a show of hands for

Bowell-Mouvemont to remain President of the Unusual Travel Agency. Anyone running gift shops is *not* allowed a vote.'

Only three hands were raised: Alfie's, Derek's, and the Professor's.

'Then by five votes to three I declare myself President of the UCC,' Nanbiter roared.

Behind him, gorilla-man grunted, 'Can I frow 'em all in the circle now, m'lud?' he asked.

Rat-face clapped his hands. 'Oh yes,' he cackled. 'Marvellous idea. Throw the weevil-fingered, puke-faced backside-wagglers through the circle to Bewayre, my lord. See how *they* likes it.'

'No, Pance,' said Sir Willikin, his face breaking into a spiteful smile. 'Not yet, at least. I don't see why we should clear *my* house of their rubbish. *They* can do it. Let us have a bonfire.'

'*Brilliant* idea, m'lord,' squealed the rat-faced man named Pance, dancing a little jig of delight. 'I don't know how you comes up with them. It's a bloomin' marvel.'

'Well then, what's it to be?' Sir Willikin said,

looking from Alfie to the Professor. 'Will you stay in the Unusual Cartography Club and obey my orders, or shall I have Bernard throw you into the circle, to live out your miserable lives on Bewayre?'

'Bewayre,' Derek growled. 'I'll never . . .'

'*Shh*, Derek,' said Alfie. He looked up at the Professor, whose moustache was fluttering with emotion. 'Can he do this?' he asked.

The Professor nodded. 'The old UCC rules are clear,' he mumbled. 'Nanbiter has more votes, so he's the president. We're up the creek without a poodle.'

'Paddle, Professor.'

'I'm fairly sure it's poodle, Rupert.'

'No, it's paddle. How would a small dog with a funny haircut help if you were up a creek?'

'Poodles are famously skilled at helping sailors in danger.'

'No they're not. They're famously skilled at being tucked under rich women's arms.'

'Oh, I must be thinking of another dog.'

'No, you're thinking of a padd—' Alfie began.

'We're up the creek without a chihuahua,' the Professor said, cutting him off. 'By UCC rules, Sir Willikin is the new President.'

CHAPTER SIX
BONFIRE OF BROKEN DREAMS

Sweat ran down Alfie's face, leaving trails of soot. Groaning under the weight of UTA brochures he staggered along a corridor. Around him the Unusual Travel Agency lay in tatters. Broken lights hung from the ceilings. Broken shelves and shattered bottles of Hoodwink's perfume (Unpleasant Burning Sensation, by Prince Hoodwink) were all that was left of the gift shop. Ripped paintings lay scattered on the floor. Past leaders of the Unusual Cartography Club smiled up at Alfie from smashed frames: Mavis 'the Yeti' Bentlegg, her hand on a globe of Mostly Eels, the first of seven planets she had discovered; Samuel

Sossigely, pictured in his specially-designed explorer's wheelchair holding a telescope up to his eye; Dolly Twutsmith, author of the first *Cosmic Atlas*, pictured in the UCC's library, proudly holding a copy of her book in one hand, and a parsnip in the other. Alfie didn't know why.

'Faster, boy,' bellowed Sir Willikin Nanbiter, poking him between the shoulders with his walking stick. 'When you've finished burning your filthy brochures, you can throw these pictures on the fire.'

'But . . . but they're nothing to do with the UTA. They're old presidents of the Unusual Cartography Club. *Amazing* people,' said Alfie. Thinking for a moment, he added, 'Well most of them were amazing people,' under his breath. 'Not *you* though.'

'*Pah*, a bunch of prancing dandy-prannets,' Nanbiter replied, giving Alfie another jab. 'Molly hats and pudding wobblers, the lot of 'em. None of them fit to rule the great UCC. Under my stern hand it will once again become a *secret* society.'

It's worth taking a small detour here. As readers returning from Book One will know, the Unusual Cartography Club was a very old society—the seventy-ninth oldest club in the universe to be exact—but hardly anyone knew about it.

Despite what Sir Willikin believed it was never

exactly a *secret* society though. Its members just didn't talk about it much, mostly because whenever they *did* talk about it people gave them funny looks. Try this simple experiment: next time you're invited to a party, open a conversation by saying, 'Hullo, I spent last week mapping planet Foopsie-Snaggleproink. They have pink hamsters with three bottoms there, you know.' Funny looks, right? And no more party invitations. UCC members learned to keep their adventures quiet and so the club became sort-of-secret by accident.

'But why does it have to be a *secret* society?' Alfie protested. 'Look, Sir Willikin, you haven't let us explain. The UCC was *dying*. There was no money left and the house was about to be demolished. The Professor and I *saved* it. Besides, the circles were *supposed* to be used by everyone. Back in the distant past people everywhere used them to travel the universe . . .'

'Siiii-*lence*,' roared Nanbiter. 'Bite thy tongue boy or I'll pull it from your head. Only a chosen few—the enlightened and fabulous—learn the secrets of the Unusual Cartography Club. And you dare tell me that I should let any mucky urchin with a handful of pennies share our mysteries. I say no,' he jabbed Alfie with his stick to make his point. 'No!' Jab. 'No, no no no *NO!*' Jab-jab-jabbity JAB.

'Ouch,' said Alfie, kicking a door open.

JAB.

'And if anyone's a molly hat it's *you*,' Alfie muttered.

A bonfire burned on the cobbles of the stable yard outside, flames leaping into the grey sky. Alfie blinked back sudden tears. Up until an hour ago he hadn't known that Number Four, Wigless Square, even had a stable yard. Now it was being used to burn his dreams. Brochures, posters, t-shirts, business cards—everything connected to the UTA—were being thrown on the fire. A picture of Prince Hoodwink blackened and curled in the flames. Polished metal letters that had once spelled **UNUSUAL TRAVEL AGENCY** lay in a jumbled heap where they now spelled out **UNRULY AUNT CLEAVAGES**. Betsy had been tossed into a corner.

Alfie's hope, too, was burning. The new stone circles he had planned for cities around the world were dying in Nanbiter's flames. Tourists who might have travelled to distant corners of the universe would never know what adventures they may have had. His universal travel guide would never be published.

Another jab from Nanbiter's walking stick sent Alfie tottering forward. Squeezing his eyes shut, he threw his armful of brochures onto the bonfire.

'*Heh, heh, heh,*' chuckled Pance, stirring the fire with a stick. He grinned at Alfie through boiling smoke, one eye bulging behind ancient specs. 'You should see the look on your face, you snivelling jam-nancy. It's a hoot.'

Hands bunching into fists, tears pouring down his cheeks, Alfie forced himself to turn away.

The donkey peered over the stable door, looking as depressed as Alfie felt. The Professor leaned on a spade beside a heaped pile of poo, groaning with one hand on his bent back. 'I must protest, Sir Willikin,' he barked. 'I *do* have a bad back you know and this corset can't take the strain. Under the Health and Safety Act of 1967 I am entitled to . . .'

'You're entitled to shut your gob,' Sir Willikin bellowed. 'Get back to work.'

'That's right, Sir W,' cackled Pance. 'You tell 'im. The chicken-legged pillow-fluffer.'

'Be silent, Pance.' Again, Nanbiter's walking stick prodded Alfie. 'You, back to work, too. There's plenty more to burn.'

Gritting his teeth, Alfie turned and trudged back inside the house. With Nanbiter poking him on, he passed the door that led down to the stone circle cavern. It had been nailed shut, and hung with chains and padlocks. The gorilla man—whose name, Alfie had learned, was Bernard Stiltskin— stood outside. 'Guardin',' he rumbled, snapping off a salute and hitting himself in the eye.

'Well done, Stiltskin. These traitors cannot be allowed into the circle cavern,' said Nanbiter, poking Alfie in the back again. 'Oh yes, I know what's going on in your crooked mind, boy. Off to Outlandish as soon as my back's turned and return with the rest of the girl's horrid tribe, eh? Couldn't win a fair vote so you'll try and *throw* us out, eh?'

Alfie groaned to himself. Sir Willikin was right: he had been thinking almost exactly that. He had friends on Outlandish: the noble hero Sir Brenda of Verminium, Prince Hoodwink's best friend—a dumb-but-cruel elf named Sparklelegs— villainous hairdresser scum and a restaurant-owner and studded leather shorts fan called Gerald Teethcrusher. All of them would have come to help throw Sir Willikin out of Number Four, Wigless Square, if Alfie could only get to the circle.

'Oh dear, oh dear, oh dear. And it's Earth's only working stone circle, eh?' sneered Sir Willikin.

Earth's only working stone circle.

The words echoed around Alfie's head. Nanbiter's stick jabbed him in the back again. He barely felt it.

Earth's only working circle.

Wheels and cogs in Alfie's brain began spinning. An idea clicked into place. He and the Professor had escaped Outlandish by finding another circle. Could they use the same plan to escape Sir Willikin Nanbiter?

Was the circle in the cellar beneath Number Four, Wigless Square *really* the only working stone circle on Earth?

More cogs spun. Chains and pulleys set off a mechanism. Somewhere deep, deep in Alfie's memory a drawer popped open. A grabbing device riffled through the cards inside and plucked one. Whirring, it passed it up to the front of Alfie's mind. He brushed dust off and took a look, a smile creeping over his face. Turning the memory this way and that, he stared at it from every direction.

Alfie's smile grew wider.

The answer to his question wasn't a proper 'no' but it was a hopeful 'maybe not'.

Let's take a quick break there. As discussed in Book One, in the misty distant past Earth had been a popular tourist destination famous for its fresh air, clean beaches, and adorable dinosaurs. A lot of circles had been needed to cope with the holiday crowds. They were still scattered all over the planet, but—as Sir Willikin said—none of them worked any more. Bits had fallen off. People had carried stones away to make interesting garden features. But Alfie's stupendous brain had shown him a glimpse of *another* circle. It was a small one—yes—but it had been built only a few years ago and every one of its stones was in the right place. As far as Alfie knew no one had ever tried using it to cross galaxies, but there was no reason it wouldn't have same power as every other stone circle.

Alfie blinked. Another stone circle meant that he could go to Outlandish and return with enough friends to throw Sir Willikin back to Bewayre. His smile widened even further at the thought. He chuckled.

'What are you laughing about, you witless dangle-drool? What nasty little worms are wriggling in that splat of dog doings you call a brain?'

Nanbiter's voice rasped with suspicion. Alfie stopped giggling. The last thing he needed was Sir Willikin watching him too closely before he could set his plan into action. He needed a distraction—fast. Wiping the smile from his face, he said, 'I was just imagining you sitting on the toilet, Sir Willikin, having a poo the size of a badger.'

Alfie squealed as Sir Willikin's stick connected heavily with his backside. 'You dirty little filth-ploppet,' Nanbiter roared. 'I'll thrash you to the other side of Tuesday.'

'Yee-ouch,' squawked Alfie as Nanbiter's stick spanked him again. Picking up speed, he stumbled along with Nanbiter close behind, his stick swishing. The explosion of bum pain was worth it, he told himself. Whatever else Sir Willikin was thinking about now, it wasn't Alfie plotting. Despite his quickly-bruising bottom, Alfie grinned again. There *was* another circle on Earth—one that Sir Willikin had no way of knowing about—and it might just be in full working order.

CHAPTER SEVEN

THE STONE AGE PROJECT

PRESIDENT NO. 897
Sir Willikin Nanbiter (1542-1546)

Commonly known as 'That Utter Git', Sir Willikin is number three in the UCC's Worst Presidents of All Time hit parade. He controlled the club for four years, with his cronies Lady Gardenia Nanbiter, Incontinence Pance, and Bernard Stiltskin. At a secret meeting it was eventually decided that he had to go. As all Presidents must map at least one new world, Sir Willikin was told of a newly discovered stone circle on an unmapped planet. There, he was told, time travelled at a very slow speed compared to Earth. Certain that he and his expedition would be back in time for dinner, Sir Willikin set off. At his departure there was much celebration and a highing of fives.

Thusly, Sir Willikin was tricked into mapping the dreadful world of Bewayre where time, in fact, moves extremely briskly. One day, in a few hundred years or so, he and his expedition may return. The next President—the delightful Emily Fuffkin—decided that was fine, so long as he wasn't her problem. If you are reading this because Sir Willikin has become your problem, good luck with that. We mentioned he's an utter git, didn't we?

Number Four, Wigless Square's library clock chimed three while Alfie read by the light of a dribbly candle. This was the only part of the house left alone by electricians and decorators, or during Sir Willikin's rampage of destruction. Alfie and the Professor had agreed they both liked it just the way it was—untouched by the centuries passing outside its door. Even Nanbiter had grunted approval at the sight of it. Nothing had been ripped out to throw on the bonfire. The golden light of Alfie's candle glowed on armchairs of cracked red leather, cobwebs, yellowing maps of forgotten planets, and the dusty spines of row upon row of books.

The door creaked open. Shutting the heavy copy of *Presidents of the Ancient and Unusual Cartography Club, Volume XII*, Alfie looked up. The Professor crept into the room, followed by Alfie's mum, and then Derek. 'Sorry we're late,' his mum said. 'Derek refused to come out of her room until we promised she could dance around in Sir Willikin's guts, singing Jamie Fringe songs.'

'I'm going to stick my foot so far up his backside I'll be wearing him like a shoe,' Derek growled, nodding.

'Then step right in,' Alfie told her, wincing at the pain in his own Nanbiter-thrashed bottom. 'This could be your lucky night.'

'Awesome,' said Derek, climbing onto a desk and sitting cross legged. Pulling her dagger, she tested it on a thumb and held it up so the blade glinted with reflected candlelight. 'First, I'm gonna stick this right up his gadzooks,' she murmured.

Alfie rapped on the table. 'Let's get this meeting

started,' he said. 'The bad news is the UTA is supposed to open in less than a week. Nanbiter is now President and we don't have enough votes to get rid of him. He's also locked the circle room. There is good news though. I've just found out that Pance's full name is *Incontinence* Pance, like the rubber knickers.'

'Names like that were common back in ye olden days,' the Professor told him. 'There was once a member of the UCC called Widdling Ninny, and another named Stop-Doing-That-At-Once Jones . . .'

'It's still hilarious,' said Alfie, grinning.

'Eh?' said the Professor. 'Why?'

'You're not helping, son,' his mum chipped in. 'These people can't just walk in here and take over. It's *your* house, Professor. We should call the police. *They* can deal with him.'

'Ah,' said the Professor. 'Sorry to sneeze on your cream bun, Mrs Rupert's mum, but that might be a teeny bit not-at-all-possible. Even if the police believed some very annoying folk from Elizabethan times had turned up from another planet the house belongs to the Unusual Cartography Club, you see.

Not, in fact, to *me*. Who was in charge would have to be decided by a judge and by our own rules he *is* the official President.'

'I have a plan . . .' Alfie began.

He was interrupted by the Professor banging a fist on the table. 'But Nanbiter has to go,' he snapped. 'Did you see his ghastly wife shovelling chow mein into her snaggle-toothed face at dinner? And the rest of them, too. My third-best tablecloth is *ruined*.'

'Yes,' Alfie agreed, 'Like I said, I have a pl—'

'It was *such* a lovely tablecloth,' the Professor murmured, tears shining in his eyes. 'Little bluebells and daffodils around the edge.'

'I'm trying to tell you, I *have* a plan,' Alfie said.

'Does it involve violence?' asked Derek.

Alfie nodded.

'See, this is why you're the brains of the operation,' Derek grinned. 'Pulling Nanbiter's lungs out through his nose and beating him round the head with them is a simple, effective, and entertaining way to solve all our problems.'

'Alfie!' squealed his mum. 'No violence! What

are you *thinking*? You know you'd lose a fight against a bag of muffins.'

'Oh yeah. I forgot about that. You're *rubbish* at fighting,' said Derek, sounding gloomy again.

'Thanks, both of you,' said Alfie, rolling his eyes although his mum was—in fact—quite right. He might be able to take on *one* muffin in a punch-up but no way was he a match for a whole bag. 'But we won't be alone. We're going to get help. From Outlandish.'

'Marvellous,' said the Professor. 'Just the sort of bold scheme I'd expect from you, you clever young sprout. But you haven't told us how you're going to get Nanbiter to unlock the circle room so we can pootle off to Outlandish. That's the part of your tremendous plan I'm really looking forward to.'

'That's the clever bit,' said Alfie, rummaging in the rucksack at his feet. Pulling out an old pamphlet, he slapped it on the table. 'We're not going to use the circle downstairs. We're going here instead,' he said, then added 'ta-da.'

Derek gave him a look. 'Ta-da?' she said. '*Really?*'

'Yes,' said Alfie. 'Ta-da.'

'Twonk.'

'Just look at the pamphlet, Derek.'

By the flickering candlelight his mum, Derek, and the Professor bent their heads over the little booklet. On the front was a photo of a hairy man dressed in a leather tunic and carrying a stone axe. In large letters across the top, it read '**THE STONE AGE PROJECT**'. Beneath, smaller letters spelled out 'City Museum: Exhibition Hall 289B'.

'I don't see how a trip to the museum is going to help . . . WOW,' his mum said as Alfie opened the booklet.

Inside was a photograph of a stone circle. Alfie tapped the paragraph of text underneath it.

The Stone Age Project was formed when volunteers from around the country agreed to spend five years living as ancient Neolithic people. During that time they built a small stone circle in an attempt to understand how such a difficult engineering feat was achieved thousands of years ago. The circle was modelled exactly on Stonehenge and later moved to the City Museum where visitors can now learn the secrets of its construction.

'We went to see it on a school trip a couple of years ago,' Alfie told her. 'Dicky Brown spent most of the day pulling my underwear over my head, so I didn't take much notice at the time but I still had the pamphlet in my school stuff. The best thing about it is that Sir Willikin has no idea it even exists so he'll never guess what we're up to.'

'I say!' the Professor squawked, staring, pop-eyed, at the photograph and tugging his moustache. 'I say! I mean to say . . . I *say! Amazing* work, Rupert. We'll just pop along to the museum and Bob for uncles. Once again you've saved our beer can.'

'Bacon. Can you make it work, Professor?' Alfie said. 'Will it get us to Outlandish?'

From behind them came the sound of someone nervously clearing their throat. Alfie's, Alfie's mum's, Derek's, and the Professor's heads snapped round.

'*Wah,*' Alfie choked.

Sir Willikin's son shuffled out from the darkness between two rows of shelves, a large book cradled in his arms. He coughed again.

'Got a frog in your throat, young fellow?' said the Professor.

The boy shook his head.

'Would you like one?' said the Professor, patting his pockets. 'The squeezed Mankpovian moistfrog is an excellent cough remedy. I believe I have one about me, somewhere.'

'Don't give him anything,' Alfie snarled. 'He's a *spy*.'

'I-I'm not s-spying on you,' stammered the younger Nanbiter, trembling in the candlelight. 'I was just t-trying to . . . to say that you may have found another s-stone circle, but it won't do you any g-good.'

CHAPTER EIGHT

FLEM

'What are *you* doing here?' Alfie gasped. 'And more importantly, how *long* have you been here?'

'I've been here all n-night,' said the boy. 'I love books, though I've only ever read th-three of them. I was born on Bewayre and the expedition didn't take many.' Looking around the library with big eyes, he continued, 'This place is a d-dream come true.'

'Yeah, right,' Alfie snorted. 'A likely story. You're here to spy on us, and now you know our plan.'

'Alfie. Don't be . . .' his mum began.

'What's your name?' Derek interrupted.

'F-Flemming,' said the boy, quietly, looking at his feet again. 'My name is Flemming Nanbiter. Though everyone calls me Flem.'

'I am Hunter-Of-The-Vicious-Spiny-Dereko-Beast. You may call me Derek,' said Derek. 'What makes you think that kicking your dad's butt back through the circle won't help?'

'You don't know him,' said Flem, looking up and pushing blond hair out of his face. 'He *never* gives up. Send him back and he'll just find a way to return, with an army of snot-crusted cannibals if necessary. Send him *anywhere* and he'll find his way back. Then he'll dish out *punishment*.' Flem took a deep breath before finishing: 'The only way to get rid of him is to use the rules he loves so much against him. You'll have to *break* him.'

'Why are you telling us this?' Alfie snorted. 'Why would *you* want to help us?'

'Rupert,' said the Professor, quietly. 'Let the boy speak.'

Alfie ignored him, staring daggers at Flem Nanbiter. 'I see through your evil scheme, Flemming Nanbiter—if that's even your real name.'

'Of *course* it's his real name,' Derek said. 'Stop being such a massive pranny.'

'Hmm,' Alfie said, crossing his arms. 'Go on then Flem. How do we *break* your dad?'

'*Vote* him out,' said Flem, his voice urgent. 'Give members the choice between him and his secret UCC or the Professor and the Unusual Travel Agency. He thinks he's always right. He thinks he's the best President the UCC ever had. If the Professor wins it will *crush* him.'

'Ahh . . . yes,' said the Professor, tugging his moustache again. 'I like your style. Of course I do. But I believe I may have spotted a teensy-weensy problemette with your plan, young Flemming.'

'So you can remember *his* name,' Alfie sighed, before turning back to Flem. 'The Professor's right. Voting didn't go so peachy last time. Because apart from you, your family, *Incontinence* Pance . . . ha . . . and Bernard Stiltskin, the only three members of the UCC are in this actual room.'

'Then bring more home,' said Flem. 'I found this on the shelf back there.' Stepping forward, he dropped the book he was carrying on the desk in front of Alfie. It landed with a dusty *thunk*.

Turning it around so the title faced him, Alfie

looked down. The book wasn't a proper printed book; it was more like a leather-bound, six-inch-thick diary, stuffed with notes and scraps of paper. On the cover someone had written the words 'Lost Members of the Unusual Cartography Club.'

Alfie gawped at it, sitting up a little straighter.

His brain caught the scent of Flem's idea like a bloodhound pressing its nose to a burglar's dropped glove. Snuffling the ground, it bounded off on the chase. Lost members of the UCC were still *members*. Like Sir Willikin and his crew, by UCC rules they could still vote if they ever returned. All Alfie had to do was find a few and bring them home. 'Exactly how many members have gone missing over the years?' he asked, eagerly.

'Oh lots,' said the Professor. 'The UCC lost people like a leaky . . . umm . . . what do you call those things? You put vegetables in them. There's a word . . . Sounds like "sieve".'

'A sieve, Professor?' said Alfie's mum.

'Yes please, apparently mine is leaking. How kind. What was I saying? Oh yes . . . the UCC lost a *lot* of people. It's why I was the last member left. Expeditions set off and were never seen again. Sometimes they got lost. Sometimes they got eaten by horrible aliens. Sometimes they just didn't *want* to come back. There are some very pretty worlds out there, and some very pretty people on them, too. Young Jammy Snuffgarden, a dear *dear* friend, met a delightful woman on planet Spudney and settled down there. They had six children, you know, all named Spiggot. Well, it's the tradition on Spudney to name . . . '

'And all the lost members are recorded in this book?' said Alfie.

'Yes, every lost expedition and every lost member was properly noted,' said the Professor. 'Spiggot, Spiggot, Spiggot, Spiggot, Spiggot, and Spiggot. Lovely children. I used to read them stories while they plaited my ear hair . . .'

Alfie talked over the Professor, his mind racing. 'So . . . If we could round up just a few lost members of the UCC and get them to vote for *you* to be president, Professor, then by the UCC rules he loves so much, Nanbiter would *have* to leave.'

'I say, that's an *excellent* idea,' the Professor

squawked, abandoning his story. '*Exactly* what I've come to expect from the splendid brain of Rupert . . . umm . . .'

'*Alfie*, Professor.' Even though he didn't like Flem Nanbiter, he was—at heart—a fair boy, so he added, 'And it's Flem's idea, though I still don't see why we should trust him.'

'You should trust me because I *want* you to break him,' Flem whispered. 'I've been dragged around stupid Bewayre my whole life. Cold. Hungry. Only three books. No one my own age to talk to. Swimming through thick, smelly bogs infested with leeches. Being attacked by snotty cannibals. Just so he could finish a useless map of a useless planet no one would ever want to visit. I . . . I *hate* him for that.'

'Ooo-*kay*,' said Derek. 'I thought *I* had issues, but you are on another *level*, Flem.'

'*Please* go,' said Flem. 'Find your lost UCC members. Vote my father out. Open your Unusual Travel Agency. I don't care. Just don't send me back to Bewayre.'

'OK Flem,' Derek said.

Alfie bit his lip. 'Hang on,' he said. 'Even if we believe him, he still knows our plan. Once we've gone, how long before his dad thrashes it out of him?'

'Oh, that's no problem,' said the Professor, beaming around the table. 'We'll take him with us.'

'No . . . no,' gasped Flem, backing away. 'Father will *kill* me.'

Alfie almost choked. 'What? That's not what I meant at all. He can't come . . .'

'It'll do the lad good to get out in the fresh air, exploring new worlds, meeting new people and so on. You know what they say?'

'No, what do they say?' asked Flem.

'I have no idea. Something about prawns, probably. Anyway, join us on our daring quest across the universe, young Flem. We'll deal with your old dad later. Toot toot, eh? It'll put pears on your . . . ahh . . . vest.'

'But you can trust me. I won't tell father where you've gone,' Flem protested. 'I wouldn't . . .'

'All right, stay then.' said Derek. Carefully, she touched Flem's jaw. 'Just here should do it,' she said.

'Wh-what are you doing?' Flem stammered.

'If you stay here I'll have to make sure you *can't* say anything,' said Derek. 'Breaking your jaw should do the trick.'

'He'll still be able to *write*,' said Alfie.

'Good point. I'll break his fingers, too.'

'I'll come. I'll *come!*' gasped Flem.

Derek gave him a thin smile. 'I thought you might.'

'Well that's settled then,' said the Professor. 'Come along then. No time to waste. Busy, busy, busy. Let's go round up some missing members of the old UCC before Sir Willikin wakes up. We leave immoderately . . . impudently . . . impishly . . . oh blast it, we leave NOW.'

CHAPTER NINE

THE GREAT WIGLESS SQUARE ESCAPE

Alfie crept down the grand staircase into Number Four's entrance hall carrying a rucksack containing everything he thought might be needed for a long journey. This included his clipboard and notebook, the *Lost Members of the Unusual Cartography Club*, a copy of Jarvis O'Toole's latest novel, which was called *Empire of Stains*, a toothbrush and—because he was a boy—only one spare pair of pants. Outside, broken street lamps fizzed. Flickering orange light poured through the diamond-paned windows. Ahead was the front door. Beyond lay a quest across the city to the museum, then across the universe, to find lost members of the UCC. Shouldering his rucksack, Alfie smiled to himself. He was the kind of boy who loved a good quest. Because he was also the kind of boy who was quite clumsy, he bumped into a chair.

'*Shh*,' squeaked Flem Nanbiter as it fell over with a crash. 'You'll wake Incontinence Pance. He's a light sleeper.'

Alfie couldn't stop a giggle. 'Incontinence Pance,' he murmured. 'Am I really the only one finding this funny?'

'There's a time and a place son,' whispered his mum. 'This isn't it.'

'Oh, I get it now,' whispered the Professor. 'Incontinence Pance, like incontinence *pants*: the rubber underwear for people with problems in the toilet area. Oh yes, *very* funny young Rupert. Well, it would be if I—like many people—wasn't cursed with a weak bladder. It's no laughing matter, you know.'

'Sorry Professor,' Alfie whispered, blushing in the dark. 'I didn't know that.'

'There was one occasion I was meeting the

Slightly Bouncy President of the Three Moons of Huhfufahfaa. I just couldn't hold on and . . .'

'Professor,' said Alfie's mum, 'we have to go, *now*.'

'That's exactly what I said, on Huhfufahfaa. Ended up using a pot plant in a dark corner, except—of course—it wasn't a pot plant at all. It was the Hobduran alien ambassador. They look a lot like pot plants, you see, the Hobdurans.'

'It's a fascinating story, Professor,' whispered Alfie's mum. 'Disgusting, but fascinating. We really do need to leave though.'

'Oh, yes, I forgot—we're escaping,' the Professor said. He paused, and then squawked, 'Wait! We can't go.'

Alfie turned. 'What? Why? We have to leave *now*. It's almost dawn.'

'*Betsy*,' squeaked the Professor. 'I can't go without Betsy. It . . . it wouldn't be right.'

'She's just an old moped, Professor.'

'But we've travelled across hundreds of worlds together. I *always* take Betsy. I'm not leaving without her,' the Professor insisted, folding his arms.

'All right,' Alfie sighed. 'We'll get Betsy. Let's try not to wake anyone, shall we?'

On tiptoe, the five escapees crept down corridors, towards the stables.

'Quiet,' hissed Flem, when Alfie stepped on a broken picture frame, glass crunching beneath his trainers.

'Just to be clear,' Alfie hissed back. 'I don't want you along.'

'Then we agree on something, I don't want to come.'

'Flem might be useful,' Derek whispered. 'I mean, you're not much good at quests, are you, Alfie? Back on Outlandish you wet yourself a little bit, didn't you?'

'It was just a *very* little bit,' Alfie hissed back. 'And there was a *dragon*. A great. Big. Fire-breathing. *Dragon.*'

'Quiet, Alfie,' whispered his mum.

'But you still laugh at people with bladder control issues,' Derek murmured. 'Despite the fact that you wet yourself over one tiny little dragon. It's sad, really.'

'And you, sweetie,' said Alfie's mum. '*Shhh.*'

Muttering to himself, Alfie opened the door into the stable yard.

Betsy—freshly polished by Derek—glittered in the moonlight where she had been thrown. The Professor *meeped* a small cry of delight. Alfie took a quick look around. Everything was still and almost silent. Only the distant rumble of night buses could be heard.

'Grab her and let's go,' he whispered, picking up a spare can of petrol that had been flung out onto the heap and tucking a helmet under his arm. '*Quickly.*'

At the sound of his voice, the donkey's head appeared above the stable door. Alfie's eyes widened as the she tossed her head back. Lips curled back from yellow teeth.

Alfie mouthed the word 'Noooooo. . .' as a sad, honking and *very* loud EEEEEE-YOOOOOORE echoed around the yard.

EEEEEEEE-YOOOOORE.

Above, a window crashed open. Sir Willikin's voice bellowed, 'What's going on down there? Shut your ugly face, Buttercup.'

Buttercup took no notice. Throwing her head back, she eeeyored again.

'I said be silent, you stinking, filthy-bottomed fleabag. *Gaaaah . . .*' Nanbiter's voice trailed off as he caught sight of the Professor.

'Oh, good evening, Sir Willikin,' the old man said. He gave Nanbiter a friendly wave, then thought better of it. Putting his hand down, he said, 'Hmm, awkward. Caught green-fingered, eh? Ahh . . . I don't suppose you could tell yourself this is all a dream and pop off back to bed, could you?'

Sir Willikin goggled, his jaw hanging open. His eyes swivelled from the Professor to Alfie to Alfie's mum to Derek and, finally, his own son. The escapees in the stable yard stared up in silence. Sir Willikin stared down, his face turning purple.

No one moved.

The Professor broke the silence. 'I say,' he said. 'Is that *my* dressing gown you're wearing? It *is*, isn't it? Of all the cheek! I'll have you know . . .'

'*Stiltskiiiiin*,' Sir Willikin bellowed.
'*Paaaaaaance*. Wake up! WAAAKE UP! Escape!
Mischief and naughtiness! Treachery! Will you
wake up, blast you both.'

Lady Nanbiter's face appeared at the window.
Without her wig, she looked like an angry
turtle. 'What is it, Willikin? What's going on . . .
Flemming? Is that you? What are you doing with
those *dreadful* little people?'

'I . . . err . . . oh . . . hullo Mother,' Flem
yelped. 'I . . . w-was just . . . that is . . . help,
help, I'm being kidnapped!'

Alfie shot him a dark look, and hissed, 'Maybe
we should—y'know—*not* stand around chatting.
Maybe we should leave. Like, as fast as possible.'

'Yes. Yeeeeeeeees,' the Professor replied,
straddling Betsy and kicking the starter. 'That's
probably for the best. Mrs Rupert's mum, perhaps
you'd like to climb on? The young folk can run for
it. Don't forget a helmet. Safety first.'

Alfie tossed his mum a helmet. Strapping it on,
she swung a leg over Betsy. Stamping on the kick-
starter, the Professor twisted the throttle. With

Alfie's mum peering over his shoulder, the moped shot through the door into the dark corridors of Number Four, Wigless Square.

'PAAAAANCE!' screamed Sir Willikin. 'STIIILTSKIN!'

Alfie ran. Close behind, Derek dragged Flem along by his ruff. Ahead, Betsy roared down corridors, leaving a wake of fluttering, half-burned brochures.

Bernard Stiltskin stepped out of darkness into the moped's path. He grinned, spreading massive arms to stop her.

Grim-faced beneath his helmet, the Professor twisted the throttle again, powering Betsy straight towards him. 'Game of turkey, is it?' he muttered.

'Chicken,' said Alfie's mum.

'Not right now, thank you,' the Professor replied. 'I'm a little busy. Hold on *tiiiiiiiight!*'

Realizing the Professor wasn't going to stop, Stiltskin tried to jump out of the way at the last moment. Too late. Betsy hit him in the stomach. With an '*Oof*' he fell backwards, disappearing beneath her wheels. The valiant moped powered straight over him, the Professor and Alfie's mum bouncing on her saddle. Behind, Stiltskin lay groaning, tyre tracks running down the length of his body and up his face.

'He looks *tyred*,' the Professor shouted back over his shoulder. 'If you get my little joke. Because he's lying down, you see, like he's tired, with tyre marks all over him.'

'Ha ha, Professor,' Alfie's mum squealed back. 'Please don't do that again.'

With Alfie, Derek, and Flem sprinting behind, the moped burst into Number Four's entrance hall and stopped, her engine revving. 'Derek old chap, get the door would you?' said the Professor.

'After them!' screamed Sir Willikin Nanbiter from the top of the stairs. 'Pance! Don't let them get away!'

Pance sprinted across the entrance hall, shrieking, 'I'll get you. I'll get you *all*, you bunch of sausage-fingered muffin spongers.'

Nanbiter jumped from one foot to the other at the top of the stairs. Squealing with rage, he pulled out clumps of his own hair, boil leaking yellow goo down his face. 'Get back here. I'll thrash you. I'll . . . I'll . . .'

Betsy's whining engine drowned the rest of his words. The little moped sped through the door at a top speed of nineteen miles per hour. Standing aside to let her pass, Alfie slammed the door shut, leaning back on the thick wood. Pance hit the door behind him like a wrecking ball, pushing it open an inch. Alfie shoved a wheelie bin against it and ran. Catching up with his companions, he glared at Flem and puffed, 'Help, help, I'm being kidnapped?'

'Ohh . . . umm . . . sorry about that,' panted Flem. 'I panicked. It *is* sort of true though.'

'We're not kidnapping you; we're taking you with us for your own safety. You were in terrible danger, remember?' Derek told him, keeping pace alongside with no trouble at all.

Flem looked confused. 'Was I?'

'Yes, from me.'

When they were out of sight of the house, the

Professor brought Betsy to a stop. Hands on his knees, Alfie caught his breath beneath a streetlamp. 'We hadn't even left the house and you tried to betray us,' he panted. 'I *really* don't want you on this quest, Flem.'

'Oh, take him with you,' his mum interrupted, climbing off Betsy's saddle. Rubbing her bottom (Betsy wasn't built for comfort) she dipped a hand in her pocket and held up a fist-sized diamond Alfie had once smuggled from a dragon's hoard in his underwear. 'Flem can take my place,' she continued. 'I'm not the questing type, so I'll stay with your Aunt Susan, sell this, and get decorators ready to fix up the mess as soon as Sir Willikin is gone.'

'Do we *have* to take him?'

'Oh, stop whining,' said Alfie's mum, firmly. 'Now, give me a kiss and go save the Unusual Travel Agency.'

CHAPTER TEN
MUSEUM TRIP

While the small band of adventurers pushed and
barged their way across the rush hour city Flem
stopped to gawp at *everything*. Every few seconds he
was swept away on the stream of people hurrying
to work. Derek twice hurled herself into traffic
to drag him from the path of oncoming, honking
buses. Gawping up at tall buildings and into every
shop window, he breathlessly told his travelling
companions the city was not at all what he had
expected. 'Mother said there would be heads on
sticks, with crows pecking at the eyeballs,' he
explained. 'She said I'd be ankle-deep in horse poop

while getting robbed by people with skin diseases.'

'The city's changed quite a bit since your father's expedition left,' the Professor explained. 'It's all so disgustingly *modern* now, but I remember when there were shoeless urchins everywhere. Horse droppings underfoot. Scabs, oozing pustules, and flaky skin as far as the eye could see. Happier times, young Flem. Happier times.'

'You'll still get robbed though,' Alfie said. 'Just wait a couple of minutes.'

'I see,' said Flem, spotting a window display of washing machines. 'Wow,' he gasped. 'What are these?'

With a sigh, Derek grabbed him by the ruff before he could wander off for a closer look.

Meanwhile, Alfie expertly dodged rush hour pedestrians, walking with his face buried in *Lost Members of the Unusual Cartography Club*. 'We could start by fetching your friend Jammy Snuffgarden, Professor,' he said. 'After that it says here there were two explorers lost on the planet Sweetly Blinky thirty years ago. Shall we get them too?'

'Ah,' said the Professor, holding up a finger. 'The Sweetly Blinky Expedition. I remember it well. Led by

Enid Groviller. A lovely woman but a little bit absent-minded. I don't know if you've ever met anyone like that?'

'Mmm-hmm,' said Alfie, turning a page.

'She forgot to take any map-making equipment, or any tents, or food, or her trousers. Last saw her wandering through the circle in a cardigan and her knickers. Big knickers. *Frilly*. Tried to stop her but she was a *very* determined woman, and rather deaf, too. Bad luck that she was travelling with Cabbagehead Tinkley, too. If anything he was worse than Enid. I once found him sleeping in a cat litter tray. He'd forgotten where his bedroom was, you see. The funny thing was the cat litter was *in* his bedroom. Right next to his bed, in fact . . .'

'It says here that time travels slowly on Sweetly Blinky,' said Alfie, interrupting before the Professor's thoughts got lost down memory lane. 'Slowly compared to ours, anyway. So they *should* still be there, if we can find them.'

'Oh, I tried that,' said the Professor. 'Sadly, the planet Sweetly Blinky was not well-named. Very dangerous. Even the flowers have teeth, you know.

Not really suitable for the absent-minded. Poor old Enid and Cabbagehead. Never seen again.'

'How about planet Rubadubadodo then,' said Alfie turning the page. 'Three UCC members were lost there in 1959.'

'Oh yes, that would be Limpney Scowell's expedition.' The Professor thought about it. 'Yes. Limpney was the sort of person who'd get lost in his own socks but they might still be there. Rubadubadodo's a fairly harmless world.'

'Rubadubadodo: check,' said Alfie, pencilling a tick on the page before looking up. 'Oh look, we're here. And the museum's just opening. We should be on planet Spudney for breakfast.'

After smuggling Betsy into the museum surrounded by herds of children on school trips, the four questers walked through a statue-lined corridor into a large hall filled with models of stone age people and glass cabinets containing flint tools. Most importantly, it contained a stone circle on a low platform, surrounded by a rope barrier and lit by spotlights.

The circle wasn't big. The tallest stones only came up to Alfie's shoulder, but there was no doubt that it was both stone and a circle: a perfect, unbroken stone circle much like the one at Wigless Square, only more dinky.

In fact, it was even smaller than Alfie remembered. 'Will it work?' he asked in a worried whisper.

'Let's find out shall we,' the Professor answered. 'It's a bit of a tiddler, but

if they followed the plan for Stonehenge properly it might get us across a galaxy or three.' Setting Betsy on her stand he stepped over the rope. Strolling around the stones, he ummed and aahed, prodding here and there, and gazing at odd, clockwork devices pulled from various pockets.

'As I thought, it won't have much *oomf*,' he shouted over eventually. 'There's a chance we'll be trapped, screaming, in the lower spatial dimensions for all eternity, too. About fifty or sixty percent, I should think. And it will be a bit like riding one of those fairground things . . . what do you call them . . . *strollertoasters*, hmm?

Only not like that at all. More like being dipped in hot butter and pushed through a garden hose, really. But not really like that either.'

'OK,' said Alfie. 'What are we waiting for then? Turn it on, Professor.'

'There's one itty-bitty probleroo,' said the Professor while fiddling beneath one of the stones.

Beneath his hand the circle began to hum, gently. 'The circle's modelled on Stonehenge, see, and it's set to the same coordinates.'

'Which means if we want to get to Spudney we need to spin it,' said Alfie, groaning to himself. 'And it's not on a rotating platform like *our* circle. How could I have forgotten that?' He gulped. The stone circle was small, but even a small stone circle was a heavy stone circle. It would take hours, probably *days*, to move the stones to the proper position.

As if on cue, a loud voice from the corner of the room, yelled 'HOI,' interrupting Alfie's thoughts. He looked up to see a security guard staring at the Professor. 'You with the moustache and crash helmet,' the man continued. 'Yes, you! NO touching the exhibits! Please step back behind the rope barrier, right NOW.'

The Professor skipped back over the rope, looking flustered.

Alfie groaned to himself. They were so close and yet so far. The stone circle was right in front of them but they'd never be able to take it apart, move it to the right setting for planet Spudney, then put it back together. The security guard didn't look like the sort of person who would listen sympathetically while Alfie told him about the Unusual Travel Agency's Nanbiter problem.

He felt a finger poking him in his back. He turned. 'You're the brainbox,' said Derek. 'Think of something.'

Alfie nodded, digging in his rucksack for *Lost Members of the Unusual Cartography Club*. 'Stonehenge,' he said aloud. 'Stonehenge, Stonehenge, Stonehenge. Is there anything about Stonehenge in here, Professor?'

'Hmm,' said the Professor, twiddling his moustache. 'About half-past nine, I think.'

CHAPTER ELEVEN

THE SEARCH FOR STONEHENGE

Alfie couldn't find any mention of Stonehenge in *Lost Members of the Unusual Cartography Club*.

An hour later, he was still trying to read dusty words scrawled by people whose handwriting skills were only slightly better than those of the average sandwich. It was a miracle the UCC had managed to map a single world. Most of its members had been the sort of people who couldn't be trusted to explore a bag of shopping. Alfie scanned the entry for Runcie Buttmiser, who had stepped out of the Wigless Square circle onto a water world, proudly wearing sturdy 'built-to-last-a-lifetime' concrete boots he'd invented. Wilf Spinnacre had married a snail named Jennifer on planet Spankfirmly, and never returned. Some of the entries were more mysterious. By the name of a cartographer called Rosie Bricklayer were just the words: 'small damp patch'.

As he turned the pages, centuries of Unusual Cartography Club history passed before Alfie's eyes, painting a story of courageous-but-doomed map-making, brave misadventure, and of sheer, breathtaking stupidity.

Alfie hardly noticed any of it. His finger ran down page after page after page, searching for any mention of Stonehenge.

'I say, you've been staring at that old book for *aaaages*. What *exactly* are you looking for?' asked the Professor, eventually.

'I'm *still* looking for Stonehenge,' Alfie moaned. 'If we can't move this circle, it might take us to some lost UCC members, at least. You said it's set to the same coordinates as Stonehenge, right?'

'Oh, you should've said,' the Professor told him, with an airy wave of his hand. 'Try page one.'

'What?'

'I said, I think you'll find what you're looking for on page one, Rupert,' the Professor repeated, loudly. 'Really, you could have asked. I'm not *completely* useless, you know.'

'I *did* ask . . .' Alfie stopped. Grinding his teeth, he turned three hundred pages to the first page of the book.

His eyes widened.

LOST MEMBER NO. 1
Catsic the Henge (date unknown)

The last person ever to use Stonehenge as a portal to other worlds, the legendary Catsic the Henge's final words before walking through the pillars were, 'Gaw, this place! It's flipping raining again. My rheumatism's playing up and I'm sick to death of it. I'm off somewhere sunny. Might build a shed and tinker around in it. Has anyone seen my sandals? Cheerio then, I might pop back in a few thousand years to see how the old planet's getting on.'

He never returned.

The remaining members of the Unusual Cartography Club looked at each other. One said, 'He's right, it does rain a lot here. Let's go to the city and build an *indoor circle*.'

'Catsic the Henge,' said Alfie, blinking up at the Professor. 'Who's he?'

'*Tsh*, I worry about today's education system, I really do,' huffed the Professor. 'As everyone knows, Catsic was one of the great UCC Presidents from way back in the wibbly-wibbly distant past.'

'Wibbly-wibbly?'

'Yes, I see now that "wibbly-wibbly" makes no sense at all. I'm not quite sure why I said it to be honest.'

'Whatever,' Alfie interrupted, staring at the drawing of Catsic the Henge. 'So he left through Stonehenge, but it's on page *one*. That must have been *thousands* of years ago. He can't still be alive, right?'

The Professor jabbed at the page with a finger. 'He said he'd come back in a few thousand years. Wasn't planning to drop his sprogs, eh?'

Alfie translated this to himself. The Professor probably meant 'pop his clogs', he decided, which was an old-fashioned way to say 'die'. 'Does anyone *plan* to die?' he replied. 'And even if he is still around, he's still just *one* old UCC member.

We'll need more than one to be sure of outvoting Sir Willikin.'

'You're being *extremely* negative, Rupert,' the Professor sniffed. 'All right so we don't know where the circle leads or if Catsic is even alive but let's look on the bright side.'

'What bright side?'

'Well we might get stuck in the lower spatial dimension for all eternity,' said the Professor, clapping his hands together and beaming. 'If *that* happens, Sir Willikin Nanbiter will be the least of our problems. So that's something to look forward to, isn't it?'

'Not really,' Alfie sighed, shutting the book with a snap and returning it to his rucksack. 'But I don't suppose we have much choice.'

'Have I got this right?' Flem chipped in. 'You're saying we go through this tiny circle that's never been tested and could trap us in empty space *forever*. If . . . and it's a *huge* IF . . . we make it out the other side, we have no idea what's waiting for us there and this Catsic fellow almost certainly died thousands of years ago. There's a tiny, *tiny* chance he might still be alive but even if he is he could be anywhere, so we just turn up and hope someone knows where he is?' He paused, then added, 'I want to go home. I mean, it's a *dreadful* plan. Not just bad, but really *really* awful.'

Alfie glared at him. 'Got a better idea? No, I didn't think so.'

'It *is* a ridiculously dangerous and massively stupid plan,' Derek chipped in. 'I *love* it.' Bunching a fist, she added, happily, 'I'll bonk the security guard over the head before we go, shall I? He'll only try and stop us.'

'No,' said Alfie.

'You ruin all my fun.'

Alfie looked around at the roomful of squealing, hyperactive schoolchildren waving clipboards, giving each other wedgies and tucking into packed lunches even though it was only half past nine. 'No one gets bonked on the head,' he said. 'I've got a better idea.'

'Hey,' he said, tapping a boy on the shoulder as he ran past. 'What's your name?'

'Davey Sprules,' said the boy. He looked from Alfie to the Professor to Derek to Flem until at last his eyes came to rest on Betsy. 'What a bunch of weirdos,' he whistled.

Alfie grinned. It was his lucky day. Davey Sprules was *exactly* the kind of cheeky young scamp he needed. 'Do you and your friends want some fun?' he asked, pointing to the security guard. 'All you have to do is keep him busy for two minutes.'

CHAPTER TWELVE

MR FURTWELL HAS A
BAD MORNING

The guard yipped, nervously, as a herd of children, led by Davey Sprules, stampeded towards him two minutes later. 'Err,' he gurgled. 'Umm, no. No. I'm not. That's not . . .'

It was too late. Children were already surging round him, waving clipboards and attaching themselves to his uniform with sticky hands. Within seconds he was swamped. Alfie smiled to himself, listening to the babble.

Davey peered up at the guard's name badge. 'Brilliant, your name's Mr Fartwell. *Do* you fart well? I bet you do. Go on, give us a fart. A really big one.'

'It's *Furtwell*,' snapped the guard. 'Now would you *please* move away . . .'

'His name's FART WELL,' Davey Sprules cackled over his shoulder.

'Fart well. Fart well. FART WELL,' thirty children chanted.

'It's *Furtwell*,' spluttered Mr Furtwell. 'With a "U".'

'What did people use for toilet paper in the Spoon Age, Mr Fart Well?' screamed a girl.

The guard yelped. 'I . . . ahh . . . it's Furtwell. Look, could you *please* let go of my jacket, young miss. I . . .'

'My mum says the droo-ids used to burn people in big men made of sticks, Mr Fart Smell. Is that true?'

'Can you fill out my worksheet for me? I'll give you a crisp.'

'Why haven't you got any hair? What happened to your hair? Did it fall out because of all the farting? Is that a thing?'

'I feel sick, Mr Fartwell.'

'All right, *three* crisps. I won't go any higher than

that.'

'*Please* leave me alone. I'm just a security guard,' Mr Furtwell shouted. 'You need to talk to one of the guides ... oh no ... No, don't do that, young lady ... *Please* don't ...'

His voice was drowned out by the sound of a girl throwing up, loudly.

'*Ewww*, Rashmi puked on Mr Fart Smell,' shrieked Davey Sprules. 'It's all down his uniform. That is the best thing I have *ever* seen.'

'Where are you going Mr Fartwell? We've still got questions.'

'All right, *four* crisps.'

With the children's questions still echoing in his ears, poor Mr Furtwell ran for it, leaving a trail of semi-digested tuna and sweetcorn sandwich.

'Well that worked out even better than I thought,' Alfie muttered to himself. Waving thanks at Davey Sprules, he shouted, 'Nice job.'

Turning to Derek, he grinned and said, 'P'ff P'ff mugsy wip chipolata,' in Outlandish.

Derek's eyes widened. 'Would I like to see you do an impression of coleslaw?' she said.

Alfie rolled his eyes, as he set off towards the circle. 'I was trying to say, "Not a bad idea, huh?"'

'Your Outlandish is terrible.' Derek shrugged. She gave the trembling Flem a shove towards the stone circle.

'This is a r-really really bad idea,' Flem stammered.

'Just get in there, you funny little twerp,' Derek replied, 'Don't worry, I'll be right behind you.'

'That just makes me worry *more*.'

'I'll . . . umm . . . bring up the ear, shall I?' said the Professor, taking his moped off her stand. 'We'll shove Betsy through first, hmm? Might be a bit of a squeeze.'

It *was* a bit of a squeeze, but with a ring of gasping school children and two astonished teachers watching, Betsy disappeared between two small pillars. One of the teachers immediately whipped out his phone and started filming.

'You've got a *brilliant* moustache,' Davey Sprules interrupted, pointing at the Professor. 'It looks like you've sneezed out two bears. What's *your* name? Is it as funny as Mr Fart Well's?'

'My name is Professor Pewsley Bowell-Mouvemont. I'm the President . . . well ex-President I suppose . . . of . . .'

'What's going on in here? Where's Furtwell? Why are you lot on the wrong side of the rope barrier?'

Alfie turned. Standing in the entrance to Exhibition Hall 289B stood a different security guard. Time to go, he told himself. Falling to his hands and knees he crawled and squeezed his way through two mini-stone pillars, while the guard gibbered 'Hoi! HOI! What . . . are . . . you . . . doing? You . . . you . . . cruuuugh . . .'

The last thing Alfie heard was Davey Sprules, saying 'Wait. Hold up. Rewind. Did you say your name was Bowel—'

And then everything went **bonkers**.

CHAPTER THIRTEEN
DARK LORD POOBIN

Before we land on a new planet with Alfie and the
crew, a few words about their light year hopping
journey. It was the strangest Alfie had ever made.
The circle below Number Four, Wigless Square
took less than a second to transport anyone across
the universe. There was a feeling of endless empty
space stretching out in all directions, then—a
heartbeat later—travellers walked out into bright
sunlight or rains of earwig-type creatures or
whatever the weather arrangements were on the
world they were arriving in.

Travelling through the mini-henge wasn't
like that. It was small and hadn't been built for

intergalactic travel. Using it was like driving a toddler's clown car up a motorway.

The entire universe streamed away from Alfie in dimensions the human brain was not built to understand. He tried to stand up straight but each of his legs stretched forty-six trillion miles in different directions, twisting around black holes and looping through galaxies like dropped spaghetti. It was unpleasant. Not as unpleasant as the *smearing* though. Alfie's nose drifted to the side of his head. One ear slipped down his neck, while the other escaped and charged off towards a distant nebula. His eyes came together somewhere around his left shoulder. He responded to this by saying 'Yurk'. The word popped out violin-flavoured and zoomed towards a planet of molten lava where it went into orbit.

The whole experience scored nine hundred and seventy-three thousand, six hundred and nine on the Fleet Unusuality Scale, and it lasted what felt like twelve lifetimes, though in fact it was only about six and a half minutes.

Eventually, Alfie tumbled from between the stones of a stone circle beneath a sky of comforting blue, landing directly on top of Betsy. He immediately had a bit of a lie-down, gasping up at the vultures wheeling above.

'That was *weird*,' gurgled Derek as she staggered out beside him still holding onto Flem's ruff. 'Did your legs do that thing?'

'Does my head look all right?' Alfie asked in reply, patting it to make sure everything was in the right place.

'Your ears look bigger,' Derek told him. 'But it's difficult to tell. They were pretty big to begin with. Flem, you all right?'

'Llamas,' hissed Flem. 'Swarms of intergalactic llamas. I don't even know what llamas *are*.'

'He's all right,' said Derek, giving Flem a pat on the back that sent him staggering to his knees.

'Ahh, that was refreshing,' said the Professor, wandering out from between the stones with his hands in his pockets. 'Spectacular display of llamas, I thought. So, from the fact that no one is screaming I assume we're not stuck in the lower spatial dimension.'

'Looks like it,' Alfie replied. Getting to his feet,

he shaded his eyes and gazed around. 'But where *are* we? After the odd journey, he was expecting to find himself on an equally odd world, but, in fact, whatever planet they were standing on looked like it might score a five on the Fleet Unusuality Scale. It didn't look very strange, but it didn't look very pretty either. The whole landscape had a 'blasted' feel to it. Skeletons lay in heaped mounds. Whirlwinds of dust blew across empty horizons. Above, a single sun blazed down on burned trees and blackened ruins. Nearby, a pile of rubble may once have been a castle judging by the broken statues wearing crowns that lay scattered in the dust. Apart from circling vultures, the only sign of life was a black tower in the distance. A giant slitted eyeball glowing above it and a large steaming teapot hanging over the doorway.

'It's almost as horrible as Bewayre,' said Flem, shuddering.

Alfie ignored him, taking his clipboard out to fill in a New Planet Information Sheet.

'Do you *have* to do that?' Derek said. 'You're always scribbling. It's annoying.'

In reply, Alfie waved his pencil at the distant

tower. 'I might want to put this world in my travel guide,' he said. 'That tower looks like an adventure waiting to happen. The flaming eyeball is a dead giveaway.'

The Professor peered at the tower, and said, 'Maybe whoever lives there could point us in Catsic's direction.'

'Oh yes, Catsic,' said Alfie, tucking his pencil behind his ear, strapping on a crash helmet and climbing onto Betsy's saddle. 'I almost forgot. Let's go find our lost UCC member, shall we?'

Kicking up a cloud of dust, Betsy puttered off towards the tower with Derek and Flem jogging behind.

Ten minutes later, Alfie pushed open the door, which creaked in a properly spooky way. 'Umm ... hullo,' he said, winding the translating gramophone around his neck. 'Anyone home?'

'By the soul-shattering sword of Gel-Madderly, I shall tear thee into a thousand bloody chunks with my bare teeth,' roared the man behind a counter.

'Uh-oh, here we go,' Alfie muttered, making a note. 'Grave peril. As usual.'

'Ooops, sorry . . . I meant to say welcome to
Poobin's Tea Shoppe. Old habit, eh?'

'I . . . uh . . . what?' said Alfie, looking up from
his clipboard. The speaker stood behind a counter
where racks of iced cakes had been set out. He was
eight feet tall and draped in a long, black cloak. Red
eyes stared from a bald and dark-skinned head that
was mostly chin. Inwardly, Alfie groaned at the
sight of it. The gravestone of a chin was just the sort
of thing the Professor would comment on, probably

leading to trouble. Inwardly, he started counting. One . . . two . . . three . . .

'I say, what a tremendous chi—'

'*No*, Professor,' said Alfie, automatically, still staring around the strange room.

The walls were covered with ragged war banners that still smelled faintly of blood. There was a large portrait of the hugely be-chinned man sitting on a throne made of screaming humans and a gigantic black sword in a display case. Purple caterpillars of magical light crawled along its length. Tables with checked tablecloths were scattered around the room, each with napkins and a menu in a stand. An oddly-shaped person, wearing dented scraps of armour, played a piano made of bones in one corner.

He stopped and turned to look at the new arrivals, leaving the last, screeching note hanging in the air. A few strands of long, greasy hair clung to his spotted scalp. His face was all nose and sharpened teeth.

'Umm ... what *is* this place?' Alfie stammered.

'Poobin's Tea Shoppe,' the dark-skinned man replied, looking at Alfie as if he were an idiot. 'I just said that, didn't I? Lord Poobin, at your service. Dread ruler of the Poobinian Empire, wielder of the awful sword Gel-Madderly, Beast of the Eastern Marches, and Master of the Rings of Torment.' He paused for a moment, then added, 'Retired. What can I get you folks? I made raspberry fancies fresh this morning.'

'Retired?' said Alfie, blinking in surprise. In the books of Jarvis O'Toole, dark lords didn't retire— they were sent to hideous-but-well-deserved deaths by secret kings with birthmarks who had grown up mucking out the pigs.

'Retired,' Lord Poobin confirmed. 'Ruled a dark empire with a fist of iron for a thousand years. Demonlord and boy. But I always dreamed of one day having a little tea shop, so I packed it in and opened this place.' He waved a hand in the direction of the goblin-shaped person at the piano, and continued: 'Old Grome stayed with me, of course. Well, he's been at my side since I pulled him screaming from his mother's corpse and you've got to have a henchman, right?'

'Right,' said Alfie. He glanced at the Professor, who shrugged, and turned to Derek.

'He seems pretty cool,' said Derek.

'Maybe we should ask . . .' Flem started.

Alfie cut him off with a glare. 'We've just arrived, Lord . . . umm . . . Poobin. What planet are we on? Where exactly is *here*?' he said. His stomach rumbled. 'Also, those raspberry fancies sound good.'

'This world is called Toby, young fellow. Welcome.' He snapped his fingers. 'General Grome, find these weary travellers a table.'

General Grome climbed off his stool and stalked across the room, knees bent and muttering. That is, Grome was muttering, not his knees. Only three species of alien creature have muttering knees, and goblins aren't one of them. 'Skin ye alive and feast on your floppy lungs,' Grome mumbled, pulling out a chair at the closest table. 'Sit,' he spat, shoving the chair against the back of Alfie's legs.

Alfie sat, saying '*Gah*,' as his legs were forced out from beneath him. The Professor, Derek, and Flem each scrambled into a chair before General Grome could help.

'Menu,' the goblin thing snarled, plucking it from its stand and slamming it down on the table in front of Alfie. 'Recommend the jam crumpets.' With that, General Grome stalked away.

'Well, this is nice,' said the Professor. 'What shall we have?'

CHAPTER FOURTEEN
ACROSS THE UNIVERSE

At Number Four, Wigless Square, Lord Willikin
Nanbiter stared at a rectangle on the wall. Colourful
images played across the screen: celebrities
sitting on sofas, flicking their hair and talking
about themselves. 'What foul magic is this?' said
Sir Willlikin, goggling as one held up a bottle of
perfume called *I'm Brilliant* that someone else had
made but which had her name on the bottle. The
other celebrities grinned and clapped as if she'd
done all the work herself.

'We do not know, my Lord Nanbiter,' babbled
Incontinence Pance, staring at the giggling celebrity.

He held up the remote control. 'I thought to discover the secrets of this black oblong of power by pressing the small buttons. Then the dark looking glass on the wall flickered into life. Perhaps it is a window into Hell itself. See how the demons have orange skin. See how unearthly white teeth are crammed into their heads.'

'Teef,' said Stiltskin, nodding.

'This world is brimming with dark magics, husband,' whispered Lady Nanbiter. 'There is a metal box in the kitchen that goes "ping". Who is this "Ping" of which it speaks?'

''Tis the name of some unholy demon, no doubt, wife,' Nanbiter told her, turning away from the television. 'All these naughty gadgets will be burned. For now, there are more important matters to hand. Tell me Pance, why did you let Bowell-Mouvemont slip through your fingers?'

'And where is my poor, kidnapped son?' added Lady Nanbiter, glaring from Pance to Stiltskin.

Pance grovelled, legs buckling as he bowed and scraped. 'Gone, my Lord and Lady. The ferret-fumbling, dangle-bangers disappeared into the grim world beyond The Door.' His voice dropped to a moan. 'Have you put your head beyond The Door, my Lord Nanbiter? Seen the world outside? Surely, the Earth is run by dark wizards now. Great beasts charge at you, farting black smoke from their rear ends. Towers of enchantment fill the sky. The people . . . the *people* . . .'

'What about the people?' Nanbiter demanded.

'Well, they are *clean*, my Lord,' Pance moaned. 'Not one of them has an unsightly skin problem like normal, decent folk. And such clothes they wear. Rude ankles on show, for all the world to see.'

'Ankles,' grunted Stiltskin, his tongue doing odd things around the inside of his mouth. 'I seen 'em.'

Lady Nanbiter's face paled beneath her rickety wig. 'Ankles! How dare you use such language in front of a *lady*,' she yelped. 'Husband, catch me. I am fainting away.'

Sir Willikin grabbed his wife's arm as she completely failed to faint away. 'It is *you* who have fumbled, Pance,' he spat. 'Yes, and you, Stiltskin. Go. Find them. I want Bowell-Mouvemont in my grasp. And then, I shall squeeze and squeeze . . .'

'WE INTERRUPT THIS PROGRAMME FOR A NEWS FLASH.'

Four heads turned toward the television where live images from the City Museum filled the screen. A reporter stood before the stone circle. Talking into a microphone, she said, 'This is Belle Giblett at the City Museum where strange events have been taking place. Witnesses say an elderly man, three children, and a moped mysteriously vanished into thin air by crawling through the museum's replica of Stonehenge. Is it some kind of hoax? You decide. A teacher at the scene took a video of the unexplained scene. We'll show it in a moment but first let's talk to . . .'

'See, my Lord!' Pance interrupted, pointing at the screen. 'What did I tell you? Look at her teeth.'

'Ankles,' said Stiltskin again.

'Shut your pie boxes, the pair of you,' snapped Nanbiter, staring at the screen.

The reporter continued: 'Vince Fartwell was the security guard on duty. Mr Fartwell, can you tell us what happened?'

'It's *Furtwell*,' snapped the security guard. 'With a "U".'

'Please, just tell us what happened, Mr Fartwell.'

The guard's shoulders sagged. 'I wasn't in the room,' he huffed. 'I was washing sick off my jacket.'

'Mr Whupply,' the presenter continued, turning to the teacher. 'You took the video. Can *you* tell us what happened?'

The teacher grinned, showing his phone. 'It's all on here,' he said. 'There was this old bloke. Massive moustache, he had. Like two Christmas trees had dropped out of his nose. And a moped. And three kids. They . . . they *disappeared*. Saw it with my own eyes. They . . . they crawled between the stones and *vanished*. Druids probably. Dabbling in the mystic whatnots.'

'Well, well, well,' said Sir Willikin Nanbiter, turning away from the screen. 'It seems the unholy window of Hell is not without uses. So, Bowell-Mouvemont has escaped through this little Stonehenge, has he?' Turning to face Stiltskin and

Pance, he folded his arms. 'What are we to make of *this*?'

'Ankles,' said Stiltskin, probing his own teeth with his tongue. 'Dirty, dirty ankles.'

'For crying out loud, will you stop going on and on about ankles,' growled Sir Willikin. 'It is obvious that Bowell-Mouvemont has used the circle to travel to another world. And not just any old world. If I'm any judge—which I *am*—it's set to the same coordinates as Stonehenge. Why would he do that? Unless . . .' Nanbiter stopped, then gasped. His boil erupted in fresh floods of pus. 'Catsic the Henge,' he hissed, to no one in particular. 'It's the only explanation. He's gone looking for Catsic.'

'What should I do, my Lord?' whimpered Incontinence Pance, bobbing up and down in an epic display of grovelling. 'How may I serve you at this difficult time?'

Nanbiter looked from Pance to Stiltskin. 'Both of you prepare yourselves for travel,' he rasped. 'Report to the circle cavern. I shall send you across the universe to bring back Bowell-Mouvemont.'

'And Flemming,' said Lady Nanbiter.

'Yes, yes, and him too.' Sir Willikin held up his fist, and squeezed. 'But I want Bowell-Mouvemont in my hands before this day is over, Pance. Do you understand me?'

'Yes, my Lord Nanbiter,' said Incontinence Pance, grovelling backwards. 'Very good, my Lord Nanbiter. We shall bring you the slippery Bowell-Mouvemont, to be crushed in your manly fist.'

CHAPTER FIFTEEN

TEATIME ON TOBY

General Grome jabbed at piano keys with filthy, dagger-long fingernails, crooning softly while Alfie leaned back in his chair, wiping jam from his face with a sleeve. 'That was a delicious crumpet, Lord Poobin,' he said. 'Five stars. Could we please have the bill . . .' He stopped, remembering there was only seven pounds in loose change, some fluff, and a dried sprout in the Professor's purse. Pulling his notebook from a pocket, he continued, hopefully, 'Or instead of paying, I could write a review of your tea shoppe and put it in the travel guide I'm writing. It would bring in more customers. This is a smashing spot for tourists exploring the depressing world of Toby.'

'That would be nice,' said Lord Poobin. 'We don't get a lot of customers.'

'We've had *one* customer,' General Grome muttered.

'Oh yes, we've had exactly *one* customer,' Lord Poobin corrected himself. 'Mainly because me and old Grome killed everyone, see?'

'I see,' said Alfie, as he wrote. 'And when you say *everyone*, you mean . . .'

'*Everyone*.' Lord Poobin nodded. 'Got a bit carried away with the dark lord thing to be honest. Once you start laying waste it's so difficult to stop, isn't it?'

'Yeah, you get caught up in the moment,' Derek agreed, getting up to peer into a glass case. Flem followed her.

The dark lord sighed. 'Silly of me not to leave a few souls alive to enjoy a nice afternoon tea.'

Alfie sucked on his pencil. 'Mmm hmm,' he murmured, scribbling again. 'Because what you really need after your civilization has been destroyed is a toasted bun.'

'*Exactly,*' said Lord Poobin, beaming. 'More crumpets?'

'That would be . . .' Alfie's voice trailed off as he looked up to see Derek and Flem Nanbiter peering into a display case. Flem's face had turned green, though Derek was pointing. 'Look,' she said. 'Look at those shrunken heads.'

'Just a small selection of my most famous victims,' Lord Poobin told her, modestly. 'You'll see King Feelas on the right, there. He was the ruler around these parts until I plunged his kingdom into war and pestilence.'

'Oh yes,' said Derek. 'I see you made a little crown to go on his weeny shrunken head.'

'It's nice to have someone in who really appreciates my little collection,' replied the dark lord, beaming.

'They're fantastic,' Derek replied. 'I've never been able to get shrunken heads right.'

'Erm . . . yes. They're . . . umm . . . very nice,' Flem gulped, shuffling an inch closer to Derek.

Alfie scowled as the pair of them bent their heads together for a closer look. This meant taking his attention off the Professor for a moment.

'Lord Poobin, I must congratulate you on the size of your ch—'

'Cheese puffs,' Alfie yelped. 'They're enormous. Well done.'

'I was going to say . . .' the Professor began.

'The Professor was going to ask if you could point us in the direction of a man named Catsic the Henge,' said Alfie, quickly. 'We're on a quest, you see.'

'A quest? How exciting,' said Poobin, polishing a glass. 'Takes me back to the old days. Questing all over the place I was: winning the Sword of Gel-Madderly from the Worm-Eyed Wraiths of Happel Crumbol, carving out my first little empire in howling rains of blood and fire, creating a goblin army to ravage the land. Oh, the fun we had.'

'Yes . . . erm . . . fun. So, Catsic the Henge?' Alfie said. 'Heard of him? Big beard. White robes.'

'Hmm, let me think,' said Lord Poobin, stroking his chin.

Because it was so large this took some time. The Professor watched, spellbound, and opened his mouth to speak again. Alfie kicked him under the table. 'My foot slipped,' he said quickly when the Professor squealed.

'The bloke with the beard was our one customer,' growled General Grome.

'Oh yes, of course,' said Lord Poobin. 'Very

good customer, too. He had the teatime sandwich selection and a chocolate finger. Said it was too gloomy round here though. Wandered off into the mountains. That way.' He waved a hand vaguely.

'Marvellous,' said the Professor. 'Now, about your magnificent chi—'

Alfie squeaked, and opened his mouth to cut the Professor off again. Instead, the old man was interrupted by the door slamming open. Hoping to see Catsic the Henge, returning for tea and another chocolate finger, he turned.

Relief turned to horror.

Silhouetted against the sunshine outside, while General Grome played on, were the last people Alfie had expected to see. 'S-S-S- Stiltskin. P-Pance. How . . . how?' he gurgled.

'Gotcha, yer little wrigglers,' Pance cackled, rubbing his hands together in glee. 'Thought you'd slip from Sir Willikin's precious clutches, did you? Heh heh heh.'

Derek spun at the sound of his voice, dropping into a crouch. Her hand grabbed the hilt of her dagger.

'Oh no you don't, young miss,' hissed Pance, pulling a knife of his own. With one step he was by Alfie's chair, holding the blade to his throat. 'You drop that, before I do this lopsided ferret's wizzler a mischief.'

Derek's knife clattered to the floor. Alfie gulped as Pance's arm looped around his neck. The little man dragged him to his feet.

'I say,' protested the Professor. 'I say. That's hardly fair play, is it? Rupert, he's got you by the throat, you know.'

'Yes, Professor,' Alfie croaked. 'I know.'

'Pie boxes shut, the lot of you,' snapped Pance, looking around. 'Bernard, get the Outlandish girl. *She's* the dangerous one. Nice to see you, by the way, young master Nanbiter. You're going to get a right ding round the ear from your pa, letting yourself get kidnapped.'

Stiltskin clumped towards Derek, swinging what looked like a broken-off leg from the dining table of Number Four, Wigless Square.

'Err . . . hello, Pance,' said Flem, his voice shaking. 'Look, there's been a misunderstanding.

Please, go back to my father and tell him . . . ummm . . .'

'Oh, I'll tell him all right,' said Pance, with an evil grin. 'I'll tell him we found you all nice and cosy with these lolloping great scum baskets. Imagine you'll get a lot more than a ding round the ear when I do.'

'More customers,' interrupted Lord Poobin, beaming from behind the counter. 'Welcome to Poobin's Tea Shoppe. This all looks like jolly quest business. Taking prisoners, is it? Oh, I could tell you a few things about taking prisoners. Prisoners are like teacakes, see? You have to toast them over a slow fire. Can I get you gentlemen anything? A raspberry fancy, perhaps? A set of kidney-crushers?'

'You keep out of this, chin-face,' sneered Incontinence Pance.

'*What*?' said Lord Poobin.

'Chin fairy paid you a visit, did she?' Pance giggled, before turning to Alfie and the Professor. 'Right then, you swivelling trout-wagglers, you're coming back to Wigless Square,' he continued, ignoring the spluttering Lord Poobin.

Ignoring Lord Poobin, it turned out, was a mistake.

The dreadlord was—it was true—retired. He was getting on a bit and his knees played him up something dreadful. But he had a thousand-year history of blood-drenched glory, and was the sort of person who—in his younger days— would shatter cities and send their people to pits of torment while he baked fairy cakes. '*Rude,*' he muttered to himself, reaching for the soul-sucking sword of Gel-Madderly.

The music stopped. General Grome's piano stool turned until the elderly goblin was facing the room. Grey lips pulled back from sharpened teeth. '*Rude,*' he repeated.

Pance was no longer ignoring Lord Poobin, or General Grome either. His eyes darted from one to the other.

'Ahh, I think you owe Lord Poobin and his excellent chin an apology,' the Professor chuckled. 'Dearie dearie me, you can't just go around pointing out people's *massive* chins like that, you know. *Very* bad manners.'

Pance yelped, staring up the length of Lord Poobin's magical sword. 'This ain't got nothing to do with you,' he growled. 'Grab them, Bernard. Let's get out of here.'

Too late.

Lord Poobin jumped over the counter like a vengeful shadow, magical sword flaring and ancient power glowing at the tips of his outstretched claw. At the same time, General Grome streaked across the room.

The knife at Alfie's throat disappeared. Free, he dived for the floor and rolled away. Head bobbing above a table, he watched Lord Poobin stalk across the room, surrounded by a swirling cloud of magical energy. 'Call me chin-face again,' the dark lord screamed in Pance's face, grabbing him by the front of his coat and jerking him upwards. 'Go on, I dare you.' Squealing, legs kicking, Pance flew upwards. His head disappeared through the ceiling in a cloud of dust and plaster.

At the same time, Bernard Stiltskin swung

his table leg. General Grome caught it between his teeth and bit down. The wood exploded in a shower of splinters.

Grome grinned, reaching out with long fingernails . . .

'I think we should . . . umm . . . go,' shouted the Professor.

Alfie didn't need telling twice. Grabbing his notepad, he lunged for the door, holding onto the Professor's back as the old man leapt astride Betsy and stamped on the starter. Engine whining, the old moped bumped and bounced over ancient bones with Derek sprinting alongside, dragging the stumbling Flem along behind. Alfie risked a single glance back over his shoulder. Behind them the black tower of Lord Poobin shook, its magical eye winking happily. Purple lights flashed in the window. Screams drifted across the broken landscape. Digging out his notebook, Alfie turned in the saddle and finished his review.

LORD POOBIN'S TEA SHOPPE *****

Offering a warm welcome to the ghost world of Toby, Lord Poobin's offers a selection of delicious sandwiches, cakes, buns, and fancies—all made with his own claws. Music is provided by the talented General Grome tinkling out classics such as *Hey Hey It's Torture Time* and *(I'm Gonna) Suck Your Brain Out Through Your Ear*. Lord Poobin is a charming host, and you'll definitely want to spend a few minutes looking at his souvenirs of death and conquest before throwing up in a bucket.

CHAPTER SIXTEEN
EVERYTHING'S FRIMPY

For six days the questers wound along ancient, overgrown mountain paths, below chilly peaks, searching for signs of Catsic. For six days they were attacked by starving vultures. For six nights they shivered around a campfire while Derek roasted the same vultures on a spit, poking them now and again and murmuring, 'Let that be a lesson to you,' at their rotating bodies.

'Great, he's not here,' sighed Alfie on the seventh day when they finally stumbled across Catsic's camp, high in the mountains. No long-bearded ex-presidents of the UCC were to be found; only a semi-collapsed shed and another stone circle.

'Must have decided to find another planet to settle down on, eh?' said the Professor, bringing Betsy to a stop in the centre of Catsic's overgrown camp. 'Can't say I blame him. You know what they say: eat a vulture and all day long you'll have horrible bottom problems.'

'Who says that?' Alfie, too, climbed off Betsy and rubbed his own bottom. The ride had been a bumpy one and he was feeling grumpy. The fact that after seven days of travel Flem had hardly left Derek's side didn't help. He glanced at Nanbiter's son. He had sat himself on a rock to watch Derek pluck yet another vulture.

Alfie scowled. Derek was *his* best friend.

'I do,' replied the Professor. Climbing off Betsy he kicked one of the standing stones. 'On the plus side, the circle is still working,' he continued. Hands behind his back, he walked around the stones, nudging them here and there with his foot. 'In fact, it looks like Catsic made some improvements,' he added. 'Interesting ones, too. Shall we find out where it leads? He might be just on the other side, a few steps away.'

Lifting the vulture, Derek gave it a shake. 'What do you think, Mrs Vulture?' she asked.

The dead bird's beak fell off.

'Mrs Vulture says let's go,' Derek said.

'Gross,' muttered Alfie.

'*Excellent*,' said the Professor. 'Well done Mrs Vulture. That's the spirit!'

Alfie shrugged. They had to go through the circle. The only other option was abandoning the quest, and he couldn't face another week of eating vulture while they travelled back. Besides, the Professor was right: Catsic might be just a step—and a few light years— away. 'Fire up the circle then, Professor,' he said.

'Hang on,' Flem chipped in. 'We don't know what's on the other side. We were lucky last time but it could drop us into a sea of red-hot lava.'

Alfie narrowed his eyes. 'This is *exactly* the kind of pessimistic attitude that makes me sorry we invited you along.'

'*Dragged* me along,' Flem reminded him.

'Details,' Alfie replied with a flap of his hand. 'Is the circle humming yet, Professor?'

'Now *this* is more like it.' Alfie dipped into his rucksack for a New Planet Information Sheet. 'This planet is *definitely* going in the travel guide.'

We should note here that the books of Jarvis O'Toole weren't Alfie's only interest. No. He also enjoyed the sort of sci-fi movies where doors slide open with a soft *pfffff* sound and computers say things like 'The inter-dimensional, ditrinium core will detonate in three-point-two seconds, Captain!'

The planet on the other side of Catsic's circle was that sort of planet.

'OK,' said Flem, looking around. 'So we're not drowning in red-hot lava. I was wrong about that. Where *are* we though?'

'Looks like a Zero-Magic Stage Six civilization to me,' said the Professor, peering around. 'You can tell from the spiky hair-dos.'

Again, we'll pause there because a quick explanation is needed. As we know there are thousands of planets inhabited by humans around the universe. Some worlds have a high magical field, which means people can get stuff done by waving a stick and shouting magic spells like 'bagguss on your headimuss'. People on planets with a *low* magical field—like Earth—tend to use technology to get things done instead. It takes a long, *long* time for folk wearing tree bark and worshipping small clay statues to get around to inventing spaceships though, so the Unusual Cartography Club came up with a hairstyle-based method of grading what stage of technology a civilization has reached . . .

THE UCC HAIRCUT GUIDE TO CIVILIZATION DEVELOPMENT

Stage One: Flea-infested dreadlocks.

Stage Two: Plaits and beards.

Stage Three: Wigs, wigs, and ponytails.

Stage Four: Greasy side-partings.

Stage Five: The 'Pro-Nutrimol' Age. Bouncy.

Stage Six: Spiky. Silly colours.

Stage Seven: Unbearable, know-it-all baldies.

Stage Eight: Spindly aerials receiving messages from other hair.

Stage Nine: Fully-automated robot hair.

Stage Ten: Back to wigs.

Where were we? Oh yes. Our adventurers had just reached a new planet.

Alfie looked around. Nearby, people with muticoloured hair, in a variety of strange and spiky styles, followed beeping, clanky robots around the park. One stopped near the Professor. Red lights flashed around its head casing. 'Bzzt. Frimp! Frimp-frimp frimp frimp FRIMP!'

'Eh?' said the Professor winding the gramophone around his neck. 'Why's it talking in that funny voice? It sounds like my odd uncle Roger. What's it saying?'

A girl with a purple mohican-style haircut, wearing what looked like a collection of car seat belts, peered round it. 'Hi, I'm Frimpette,' she said. 'The tourist information unit said if you don't keep off the grass it will exterminate you in three seconds.'

Her voice streamed from the Professor's small gramophone trumpet in English. She blinked at it, surprised, and said, 'Hey, frimpy translation-gizmo, frimp-pants.'

'I . . . err . . . umm . . . thank you, I *think*,' said the Professor, shuffling off the grass.

'It's the only grass left on the planet,' Frimpette said. 'You frimp me, old frimper?'

'Umm . . . yes. Err . . . frimpy,' said the Professor.

'Woah, watch your language,' hissed the girl, narrowing her eyes. 'Not frimpy, frimp-dude. Not frimpy at *all*.'

The Professor tapped his translator. 'Seems to be having trouble . . . Ahh, I see. No wonder. Your entire language is based on the word "frimp". The meaning depends on exactly how you say it and my accent made it sound like a rude word. Am I right?'

The girl raised one knee and waggled it. 'Yes,' she said.

Alfie wrote a '6' on his Planet Information Sheet and wound his own translator. 'Can I ask a few questions?' he asked.

The girl shrugged. 'Frimp away.'

'First. What planet is this?' Alfie held his pencil poised to write.

The girl stared at him. 'D'uh. Planet Frimp. Are you a frimp, or something?'

'In my language we say "twonk",' Derek chipped in.

'That's what I said—*frimp*. Wow, where did you get the frimpy bird, frimperina?'

'You can have it,' said Derek, handing Frimpette the half-plucked vulture. One of its eyes fell out and dangled from the socket. 'It's gone a bit manky,' she added.

'*Really*? That's . . . that's the frimpiest present I've ever had.' Frimpette looked like she might burst into tears. Alfie crossed out the 6 and replaced it with a 7. He'd never thought he would ever see a girl with a purple Mohican snuffling over a smelly, almost-bald vulture. 'I'll whizz it around in my Clone-o-matic LifeStarter 3000 and see what frimps,' the girl continued, tucking it under one arm. 'Maybe I can recreate the species. Planet Frimp can have birds again.'

Mrs Vulture's head flopped over to one side, peering back at the travellers through one still hate-filled eye.

'Good luck with that,' said Derek. 'They're good for a fight but don't taste very nice.'

'We're looking for a man named Catsic the Henge,' Alfie interrupted.

Frimpette goggled. 'Catsic the Henge?' she gasped.

'Yeah,' Alfie told her. 'Long beard. Likes sheds. Ever heard of him?'

'But that's impossible, frimp-dude,' Frimpette gasped. 'Catsic disappeared thousands of years ago. He's like a *total* hero. Legends say he saved the planet from a Frimpaloid space invasion and then vanished, leaving behind only these two frimpy circle things.'

'*Sheesh*,' said Alfie, rolling his eyes. 'He's not on *this* planet either.'

'Frimpaloid?' said the Professor. 'I don't believe I've heard of the Frimpaloids.'

'Death ray jelly things on stalks,' said Frimpette, her nose wrinkling. 'Planet frimpers. Nasty.'

'I could just go for a bowl of jelly after all the vulture,' murmured the Professor. 'I don't suppose they were lime flavour, were they? That's my favourite.'

At this point the tourist information unit buzzed. 'Unacceptable time delay,' it said, snappishly. 'To continue with Catsic the Henge historical tour, press A now.'

'I'd better go,' said Frimpette, jabbing a button on the robot and following it along the path. 'I'm doing a report for school. Thanks for the dead bird, frimpers.'

'Hang on,' Alfie shouted after her. 'You said there were two circles. Where's the *other* one?'

'That way,' Frimpette shouted back, pointing. 'Just past the statue.'

Alfie wandered along the pathway, slightly behind the rest of the group, staring around at the hi-tech world and scribbling notes. Planet Frimp was shiny, but—in its way—almost as depressing as Toby. Its weirdly-shaped skyscrapers and flying cars and giant holographs were pretty cool, but he missed nature. His own local park was full of litter and dog poos that lurked in the grass, waiting to throw themselves beneath the soles of his trainers, but at least the trees weren't in protective cages. The city pigeons would have your eye out and steal your chips, but they were sort-of wildlife. Planet Frimp didn't seem to have any at all.

The Professor fell in beside him. As if reading Alfie's mind he said, 'It won't always be like this, you know. In a few centuries everyone will go bald. They'll tear down the buildings and make the entire planet into a tranquil garden, then sit around—cross-legged, probably—humming and being horribly, horribly pleased with themselves.'

Alfie nodded, looking up as they passed a tall statue of the ancient UCC president. He looked very

much like the drawing in *Lost Members of the Unusual Cartography Club*, which is to say, mostly beard.

The Professor followed his gaze. 'Bit of a show-off if you ask me,' he said, peering up and stroking his enormous moustache. 'I mean, would you look at that beard. Overdoing it, really. Attention-seeking. So, young Rupert, I just wanted to have a teeny word with you about young Flem.'

'Is he getting on your nerves, too?' Alfie replied, nodding.

'Umm . . . that's not quite . . .'

'Found it,' shouted Derek from up ahead. Without waiting to hear what the Professor was going to say, Alfie hurried around a bend in the path. There, in front of him, was another circle.

Catsic the Henge

It glimmered.

'Oh my,' puffed the Professor, coming up behind him. 'I've never seen a *glass* circle before.'

DISCOVERING . . . FRIMP
_____

The sort of world that has jet packs and laser guns that go pew pew pew, Frimp is a must-visit for anyone who enjoys robots with funny voices, sky-sized holograms advertising fizzy drinks, or massive, world-spanning cities that have everything except a bit of peace and quiet.

CHAPTER SEVENTEEN

THE PLANET HOPPING CHAPTER

After leaving Earth, Catsic the Henge, it seemed, had spent decades seeking a Goldilocks planet to settle down on. One that wasn't too hot, and wasn't too cold. Not too busy or too grimly desolate. He was nowhere to be found on the next planet our adventurers visited, or the one after that either. While days slipped by and the Professor's watch showed hours ticking away back on Earth, our questers travelled from world to world, finding no signs of the ex-president except another new and improved circle leading to yet another planet. On some, Alfie barely had time to fill in a New Planet

Information Sheet before stepping into yet another circle, on others the four adventurers had to travel for weeks to find the next circle. Alfie was able to make proper notes. To save time, let's have a flick through some highlights.

DISCOVERING . . . MYTHOLOGIA

History lovers will enjoy this world, where ancient sites and legends wait around every corner. Must-see places include . . .

The Sunken City of Pratlantis

Centuries ago a devastating earthquake caused Pratlantis to sink beneath the waves, but only by about three inches. It now advertises itself as a 'lost' city, though, in fact, about 30,000 people live here and it's a popular paddling destination.

The Labyrinth of Spinelus

Found beneath the ruins of an ancient palace, the Labyrinth of Spinelus dates back to the world's most distant past. Ancient tales tell the story of the hero Spinelus, who descended into the dark maze below the palace to battle a fearsome beast: an unnatural creature with the head of a gerbil and the body of a gerbil. The site now has a small pet shop.

The Temple of Cataar

Home to the Coughing Oracle, this delightful old temple sits above a cave where thick, poisonous smoke pours from a crack in the floor, carrying visions of the future from the Underworld. For a small fee these messages are breathed in and translated by the oracle. One silver groat will get you a basic message such as 'A-cuurgh hurgh broccoli legs a-curgh hech hech a-hurrgh,' while ten silver groats buys an in-depth reading of your future that comes tied with ribbon on a phlegm-soaked roll of parchment.

WHERE TO STAY

Ocean View Hotel ★★★★

Bizarrely, the one thing the Ocean View Hotel does not offer is views of the ocean, having been built six hundred miles inland. It does, however, boast the best swimming pool on Mythologia and, one day, the owner—Spiros Hedtrawma—plans to fill it with water. In the meantime, the water slides and diving boards

are all open, though visitors are advised
not to use them however much Spiros and
his wife encourage you to do so.

Stiltz *****
This romantic collection of luxury, palm-
roofed huts has been built on stilts out to
sea, giving customers the chance to sleep
above the waves. Sadly, the builders did not
think to add walkways from the land so
visitors will have to swim to their room
through shark-infested waters. Each hut is
equipped with a petal-strewn hot tub and
visitors will enjoy the attentions of their
own—slightly chewed—butler.

WHERE TO EAT

Catch of the Day **
This delightful beachside shack proudly serves
only what the local fishermen have caught
in their nets that day. Attention is required
as the fishermen are not very good and
customers may be served highly poisonous sea
slugs, driftwood, dead seagulls, and—in season—
Kraken.

DISCOVERING ... PLANET SWETII

This exotic jungle planet is notable for its river, which spirals around the world from top to bottom. A short stroll from the town of Poorli Bellhi you'll find the spectacular Golden River Falls. Swetii's largest system of cascades and waterfalls, locals say the rich yellow waters are caused by gold dust washed down from the mountains. They are, of course, lying. The distinctive colour is due to the massive sewage outflow from Diharria City, upriver.

YELLOW-WATER RAFTING WITH BOB'S ADVENTURE TOURS

At Bob's we offer the wettest, wildest ride on Swetii! Feel the spray on your face as you *WHIZZ* down the Golden River! *SURF* down distasteful yellow scum! Stop to *SWIM* in exotic steaming jungle pools! End your trip with a fortnight stay at the Poorli Bellhi hospital!

* THRILLS! SPILLS! DEAD FISH! BLADDER INFECTIONS!*

DISCOVERING . . . GODSWORLD

Shrouded in mystery, and acid fog, Godsworld is said to be at the exact centre of the universe and is home to thousands of giant stone heads that stare into the distance, their faces set in expressions of forlorn hopelessness. No one knows exactly who carved them, or why, but legend tells that the heads represent a party thrown shortly after the world was created. None of the gods who came knew each other very well, the only food available was plain crisps and the whole thing was bit awkward. After standing around for a while, making patchy conversation about how difficult it was to create a really good world these days, the gods got their coats and went home.

CHAPTER EIGHTEEN

ALL ABOARD THE *JEWEL* OF THE *BREEZY SEAS*

Two days passed on Earth, six weeks for our brave questers as they hopped from one end of the universe to another and back again. Hungry, ragged, and getting proper cheesed off with the endless search for Catsic the Henge, they eventually arrived at the small but pretty planet of Solstice, known in the local language as the World of Ten Thousand Isles. We rejoin Alfie, Derek, Flem, and the Professor at the docks of one of its larger islands where they were standing on a jetty before a jaunty ship, its sails fluttering, while elderly passengers clutching luggage made their way up the gangplank.

THE BREEZY SEAS EASY CRUISE

Join Captain Swag and her merry crew* on the *Jewel of the Breezy Seas* for a two-week luxury cruise around Solstice's sun-drenched islands. Swig grog in style at the captain's table and enjoy our fabulous spa facilities. All cabins with en suite bathrooms and FREE, complimentary parrot (changed daily). Only 30 Silver Pieces per passenger.

PIRATE JOKES! MERMAID SPOTTING! PIPES! WOODEN LEG CARVING CLASSES!

CASINO AND NIGHTLY ON-BOARD ENTERTAINMENTS, INCLUDING . . .

* Bosun McHearty and His Happy-Legs Jig Extravaganza *
* Warbling Seaman Pete 'The Solstice Songbird' *
* The Comedy Stylings of Second-Mate Diddy Doodat *

WE HARDLY EVER SINK!

*Not all crew members are merry. Ship may contain grizzled sea dogs.

The captain herself stood by the boarding plank, a parrot on her shoulder. One of her eyes was covered in a black patch. The rest of her was every inch the jolly buccaneer, from the wide-brimmed hat with its bobbing feather to her big, leather boots.

'Umm . . . good morning . . . or shiver my fingers as I believe you salty sea dogs like to say,' said the Professor, winding his translator. 'We're looking for . . .'

'No, no, no,' said Captain Swag, slapping the Professor's shoulder. 'All wrong, matey. We start with a joke. 'Tis the way of things for us salty dogs. A sea shanty in the heart, a jig in the legs, and a side-splitting gag on the lips.'

'I . . . err . . .' replied the Professor, looking baffled.

'So I says to you, "What's a pirate's favourite letter?"' Captain Swag continued. She looked expectantly at the Professor.

On her shoulder, her parrot croaked, 'Pirate's favourite letter. The C. Aargh.'

'Shut up, Polly, you're ruining my joke,' snapped the captain. She winked at the Professor, though it might have been a blink. It was difficult to tell because of the eyepatch. 'Sorry about the parrot. He's got no sense of comic timing. If you wouldn't mind forgetting you just heard that . . . So I says, "What be a pirate's favourite letter?" And *you* says . . .'

She crossed her arms, waiting for the Professor to respond.

'We're trying to find a chap called . . . oh, what was his name?' said the Professor. 'Don't tell me. I'll get it in a moment. Umm . . .'

'Catsic the Henge,' said Alfie, helpfully.

'That's him,' said the Professor. 'I knew I'd get it. We're looking for Matchstick the Hinge.'

'Catsic the Henge,' Alfie repeated.

'Aargh, 'tis old Catsic ye seek is it?' said Captain Swag. 'He be far away from here, cast away on the Isle of Sheds.'

Alfie's heart leapt. Wide-eyed, he gasped, 'He's here? He's *really* here? On this actual planet? It's not just another stone circle?'

'Aye, old Catsic be here,' Captain Swag confirmed. '*Strange* fellow. He ain't left his island in years. They say he be haunted, by a long, wispy ghost that hangs off his chin.'

'A beard then,' Derek chipped in.

'Mebee a beard; mebee a ghost,' growled the captain in a low voice. 'A cursed spectre, doomed t' dangle from old Catsic's chin until its spirit be at peace. For do they not say that no one *truly* knows the way of ghosts, or beards?'

'By golly, if he's here, that's . . . well . . . *marvellous*,' puffed the Professor, ignoring Captain Swag's rather silly ghost-beard twittering. He opened his purse and jingled it beneath her nose. 'So, Captain, could we hire your boat for seven pounds, some fluff, and . . . if I really have to part with it . . . my lucky sprout?'

'No, no, no, no, no, *no*,' said Captain Swag, shaking her head. 'We can't haggle over the price until we finish the joke. Where were we? Oh yes. *I* say, "What's a pirate's favourite letter?" Then *you* say . . .'

'Oh,' said the Professor. 'Well, I suppose a pirate's favourite letter might be from his Aunt Lucy. My Aunt Lucy used to write some delightful letters. That was before the squirrels took her, of course . . .'

'"R",' said Captain Swag, firmly.

'Eh?' said the Professor.

'No, not "A"—"R",' the captain replied. 'You're *supposed* to say a pirate's favourite letter is "R".'

'Am I? That would be a very short letter, a bit

lacking in family news. That's how I knew about the squirrels, you know. Aunt Lucy would often write that they were watching her again.'

'*You* say a pirate's favourite letter is "R", and then *I* says, "No, his true love be the "C",' Captain Swag insisted.

'Yes, I suppose that would make sense,' said the Professor, nodding. 'Pirates do enjoy the sea, I'm told. Puttering about in boats and so on. And he's written his Aunt Lucy a letter about it, has he? Good for him. Pirates get such a bad reputation. It's nice to know they keep in touch with their elderly relatives.'

'Look,' said the Captain, grinding her teeth. 'Pirates say, "Aaargh", which sounds like the letter "R", so . . .'

Alfie sighed, tapping his foot impatiently on the wooden jetty. 'Could I interrupt?' he said. 'Really, Captain Swag, it's a *brilliant* joke but we'd just like to hire your ship.'

'Is it a *magic* sprout?' asked the captain. 'The sort of sprout that might . . . say . . . light up with a green, unearthly light when you're close to buried treasure?'

Alfie bit his lip. Telling Captain Swag the sprout had magical properties might persuade her to take them on board. He was, however, an honest boy, so he shook his head. 'It's not magic, is it, Professor?'

'No,' said the Professor. 'It's got a patch of mould that glows in the dark though.'

'So mateys, you wants me to give ye all a two-week luxury cruise for seven foreign coins what I can't spend, some fluff, and a mouldy sprout,' said the Captain thoughtfully. 'Let me think about it . . . Hmm, I've thought about it: the answer is "Get lost". You could try over there.' She pointed to the only other ship in port and dropped her voice to a whisper. 'They say it be a *pirate* ship. Which reminds me: how do pirates . . . ?'

'R,' interrupted the Professor. 'Did I get that right?'

'Well, yes. Yes, actually you did,' said Captain Swag, sounding disappointed.

Alfie glanced at the other ship and shivered. Its filthy decks were deserted, its patched sails ragged. Wicked-looking cannon jutted from portholes as if sniffing the air for enemies. Beneath its prow was a carved figurehead—a skeleton crowned with seaweed hair. Painted along the tar-black side was the ship's name: *The Plague Dolly*.

Nailed to a post next to the ship was a board of wood, painted with dripping red letters.

Join Captain Bad Hair O'Hooligan and her ~~vicious~~ Jolly crew of ~~desperate thugs~~ friendly ~~vermin~~ sailors on *The Plague Dolly* for ~~robbery and death~~ the adventure of a lifetime!

~~Firing enemies' heads from cannons!~~
Tropical island paradises! Drinks in coconuts! Umbrellas! ~~Hook hands!~~ Ear piercing! Our true love be the C!
Aargh!

WE ARE NOT PIRATES!!!

Our 100% passenger guarantee: Unlike other cruises we promise not to steal any women's clothes you may bring aboard then drunkenly parade up and down wearing them while twirling parasols and jeering as you're forced to walk the plank at sword-point.

'We'd much rather travel on *Jewel of the Breezy Seas*,' Alfie said. Captain Swag's ship looked a lot nicer. For a start its figurehead was a cheerful-looking woman who still had all her own skin, though she had lost a lot clothes somewhere.

'Well then, young shaver, come back with thirty silver pieces each,' said Captain Swag. 'Only you'll have to wait now. We set sail in ten minutes, but we'll be back in a fortnight.'

'We can't wait a *fortnight*,' said Alfie.'Are there any other ships . . . ?'

Flem raised his hand. 'Umm . . . we could work for our passage,' he suggested.

'No one asked *you*, Flemming Nanbiter,' Alfie snapped. 'Captain Swag, the Professor and I represent the Unusual Travel Agency. We could send a lot of customers your way . . .'

'Aargh, the young Jack Tar there do have a point. We could use a few extra hands on board,' said Captain Swag, squinting at the four adventurers. 'Seawoman Parts is down with the scurvy and Chicken-Neck Jon Spatula ran off with a mermaid on our last cruise. Well, *he* ran off, *she* just sort of flopped about on the jetty. It was embarrassing for everyone, really. Hmm . . . do any of ye know how to splice a main brace?'

Alfie, the Professor, Derek, and Flem all shook their heads.

'No, me neither. Anyone fancy serving customers in our Undersea Fantasy Bar and Grill?'

Four heads nodded.

'You be hired then,' said Captain Swag, putting her hands on her hips and adding a cheerful, 'Aaaargh.'

'How long until we get to the Isle of Sheds?' Alfie asked.

'We don't sail to the Isle of Sheds,' said Captain Swag. '*No one* sails to the Isle of Sheds. Old Catsic don't much like visitors. But I can drop you at the port of Tornickers. It's packed with thieves, cutthroats, and murderers, o' course, but if you kill a drunken captain in a bar brawl you could fight your way onto his ship, toss the rest of the crew overboard with knives between your teeth, and sail it the rest of the way.'

'Dibs,' said Derek.

'Welcome on board then, me hearties,' said Captain Swag. 'Before we weigh anchor, does any of ye know how a pirate cooks his meat?'

'On a baarghbecue,' screeched the parrot.

'I hate you, Polly,' huffed Captain Swag as she turned to lead the questers up the gangway. 'Like really, *really* hate you.'

CHAPTER NINETEEN
STRIFE ON THE OCEAN WAVES

Alfie stumbled across a heaving deck, carefully balancing a tray of drinks as he weaved between deckchairs. He'd stripped down to a t-shirt and rolled his jeans up, but he was still sweating beneath Solstice's suns. A sailor's life was hard. Since coming aboard *Jewel of the Breezy Seas* he'd swabbed decks, polished barnacles, and folded the ends of the toilet rolls into a nice neat triangle in every cabin.

'What time does the bingo start, young man?' asked an old woman with a face like a shrivelled spud at the back of the vegetable rack.

'After dinner,' said Alfie, handing her a Breezy

Seas Headbanger cocktail, loaded with fruit and umbrellas.

'I'm eighty-three, you know,' she replied.

Let's take a moment there, shall we? Elderly people across the universe obey certain laws. When they hit about eighty a deep instinct awakens within them: an instinct that forces them to tell everyone they meet how old they are *all* the time, as if living a long time is a competitive sport at which they are gold medallists.

'Could you give my feet a rub for me, dearie?' the old woman in the next deckchair demanded. Pulling up her blanket she waggled yellow toenails in Alfie's face. 'I got terrible bunions and I paid extra for the daily foot massage.'

Yep, a sailor's life was hard. Alfie squatted, looked down at a strangely lumpy, gnarled foot with a gulp. Squeezing his eyes closed and gritting his teeth he prodded the foot with the tips of his fingers. Questing wasn't supposed to be easy, he reminded himself. Every adventure had its moments of bone-chilling horror. These were the moments the soul is tested: the moments when heroes rise.

His face twisted in torments of disgust Alfie dug his thumbs into old-lady foot. Bone creaked beneath his fingers. Flakes of skin came away in his hand. A couple of verrucas winked at him.

'Good morning,' said Flem, walking past. 'Lovely day for it.'

'Shut up,' hissed Alfie between clenched teeth.

'*Ooo*, that's the stuff, get right in there young man,' the old lady interrupted. 'Don't be afraid to work up a sweat.' She sighed, happily. 'I'm a hundred and twelve, you know.'

Alfie did what everyone else in the entire universe does in this situation. Keeping his eyes anywhere but the foot between his hands, he whistled in disbelief and said, '*Really?* You don't look a day over thirty.'

'What a *nice* young man you are,' she cackled, beaming at him. 'When's the bingo start, young man?'

'The young man said after dinner,' said the first old woman. 'You gotta keep your ear trumpet turned on Mavis, you daft old trout.'

As is the way of old people, the two of them were asleep thirty seconds later, heads lolling from side to side with the rocking of the ship. With a sigh of relief, Alfie set Mavis's foot down, and wiped his hand on her skirt. Taking the empty glasses he backed away to take a well-deserved break. Leaning on a rail, he watched islands drift past as the ship smashed through waves. A couple of mermaids frolicked in the spray alongside. Nearby, the Professor was on his own lunch break, snoozing in a deckchair with a knotted hankie on his head and occasionally muttering the word 'hair' in his sleep. Above, sails snapped in the wind, as clean and white as the seagulls that circled the masts. With a few minutes to himself, Alfie took out his notebook and began writing a review for his travel guide.

Captain Swag's Breezy Seas
Easy Cruise *****

If a great value swashbuckling holiday on
the high seas is your thing, then all aboard
Jewel of the Breezy Seas for the trip of
a lifeti～～

That was as far as he got.

'Oi,' Derek said, jogging his elbow. 'Why are
you being so mean to Flem?'

Alfie scowled at the jagged line his pencil had
made across the page. Tucking it behind an ear he
glared at Derek, saying, 'I'm *on* my *break*.'

'Like I care,' Derek growled, crossing her arms.
'What's Flem ever done to *you?*'

'Hmm, let's see shall we?' Alfie replied. 'Oh, yes,
that's right, he voted for his git dad, didn't he? Thus
helping to destroy everything we've worked for.'
Putting a fist up to one eye, Alfie smudged away
a non-existent tear. 'Sniff,' he added. 'Squish. Bad
Alfie. Naughty Alfie.'

'He was scared,' Derek shot back. 'But he's all
right once you get to know him.'

Alfie sighed. 'You can't expect me to *like* him. He's . . . '

'Lost on the far side of space, far from the only planet he's ever called home,' Derek interrupted.

Alfie snorted. 'You weren't so nice to *me* when I was stranded on Outlandish. I seem to remember you called me a Cabbage-Eating Fartpig every time I opened my mouth.'

'*You* were different,' Derek snapped back. 'Everywhere you go it's like that's where you're *supposed* to be. You *never* seem lost.'

'So, you being nice to Flem has nothing at all to do with his Jamie Fringe hair, and cute nose?' said Alfie, raising an eyebrow.

Derek put her own nose to Alfie's, her voice an angry hiss. 'I'm trying to talk to you as if you weren't a twonk,' she said. 'But you're making it very difficult because you *are* a twonk. You don't like him: *fine*. I can understand that. I didn't like you much when I first met you either. So think about it this way: we have to get votes for the Professor to become president again, right? If this quest is successful we have four votes: you, me, the

Professor, and this Catsic weirdo. Nanbiter still has five, including Flem. But if *Flem* votes with us, that's four for Nanbiter and five for the Professor, isn't it, *twonk*?'

Alfie blinked. 'Oh,' he gasped. 'I hadn't thought of that.'

'No, you hadn't,' sniffed Derek. 'Because you are a *twonk*.' With one last glare, she turned and walked away.

'So, *that's* why you're being nice to him?' Alfie called after her. 'For the extra vote?'

His only answer was one of Derek' s rude gestures.

'Derek! Flem lash parr s'plop ploppy der-wang c-hurggh fishfinger,' Alfie shouted, trying his Outlandish again.

'You'd like to use my hat as a toilet,' Derek shouted back. *'Nice.'*

'I meant to say, "Flem's too weak to stand up to his dad,"' Alfie mumbled to himself. He watched as Derek disappeared down wooden steps into the depths of the *Jewel of the Breezy Seas*. Biting his lip, he frowned. She was right. If they had Flem Nanbiter on their side, Catsic's was the only extra vote they would need. They wouldn't have to dash about the universe trying to round up more lost members of the Unusual Cartography Club. For a moment, he stared out to sea. Flem *hated* his dad, even though he was terrified of him. Probably *because* he was terrified of him. So maybe . . . just maybe . . . he could be nudged to vote the right way.

'Young man,' called a quavering voice behind him, interrupting his thoughts. 'Coo-eee, young man. You forgot to do the other foot.'

With a sigh, Alfie tucked his notebook in his pocket and turned back to the row of deckchairs. A sailor's life was hard.

CHAPTER TWENTY
AAARGH!

DISCOVERING . . .
SKULL ISLAND

Shaped like an **enormous** skull with smoke coming out of the eye sockets, Skull Island is home to a **giant**, chest-beating gorilla. Visitors going ashore should be careful not to approach the beast as it will aggressively sell them souvenirs such as bobble-head gorillas wearing grass skirts, straw gorillas in jaunty hats, or cheeky gorilla-in-a-bikini postcards.

And so, *Jewel of the Breezy Seas* crept across a map dotted with palm-covered islands, carrying our intrepid questers on a zigzag course towards Tornickers with frequent sightseeing stops.

On board, Derek looked away from Alfie with a sniff whenever they passed in the ship's narrow passageways.

In turn, Alfie ignored Derek, while forcing a friendly smile whenever he passed Flem.

Flem wondered what was wrong with Alfie's face.

The day before they were due to reach their destination Alfie struggled down a corridor, carrying a pile of fresh sheets from cabin to cabin. Spotting Flem coming in the opposite direction with a basket of tiny soaps and miniature bottles of shampoo, he stopped. 'Hullo hullo hullo,' he said, grinning.

'Are you in pain?' asked Flem, squinting at Alfie's grin.

Alfie turned it down a notch. 'Just pleased to see you,' he muttered, adding, 'You're looking well. Tanned.'

'Yes, it's the sunshine.'

By now, Alfie was struggling. 'Talking of sunshine,' he stammered, 'have you noticed the sunsets on this planet? Very pretty. Same colour as ham when you stop to think about it.'

Flem nodded. 'Ham,' he repeated.

The friendly chat wasn't going well, Alfie had to admit. The atmosphere between himself and Flem was still as tense as an expensive glassware shop where a three-legged rhinoceros was browsing for gifts. 'So . . . umm . . . catch you later,' he said, screwing his face into what he hoped was his best smile yet.

Flem stared, shuddering. 'Are you sure you're alrigh—'

He was interrupted by a distant **BOOM**. A second later the ship lurched beneath their feet. Timbers smashed. Screams echoed down the passageway. Captain Swag's voice shouted, 'Wumph burble portly stink bag! Wumph burble pigholder!'

Dropping the sheets, Alfie wound the tiny gramophone around his neck.

'All hands on deck, me hearties. Pirates! There do be a pirate ship off the port bow. Shut your beak, Polly. For crying out loud, *will* you shut up, you hateful bird!'

Alfie raced down the corridor, Flem close behind. They emerged, blinking in the sunshine to see the captain standing in the prow with a telescope pressed to her good eye. Another **BOOM** rolled across the waves. Above Alfie's head a cannonball tore through the sail.

He ducked, running through the crowd of panicking sailors and passengers to where the Professor stood with Derek, shading his eyes with one hand and staring out over the waves.

'What's happening?' Alfie yelped, skidding to a stop.

'We seem to be under attack from saucy, Jack tar, buccanuccanuccan . . . *pirates*,' said the Professor, pointing. Alfie's gaze followed his finger. A ship ploughed through the ocean towards them, her grey and torn sails straining, her skeleton figurehead grinning.

'*The Plague Dolly*,' Alfie gasped. 'What's it doing all the way out *here*?'

'Attacking us,' the Professor repeated. 'You can tell it's attacking us because it's firing cannons at us. The cannons are *always* a big giveaway. Various folk have fired cannons at me . . . let's see . . . thirty-eight times . . . no, thirty-*nine* times including that time on planet Hinkletarrter . . . but not *once* has a cannon been fired at me in a playful, "Hurrah, here-comes-Professor-Pewsley-Bowell-Mouvemont" kind of way.'

BOOM. BOOOOOOM!

Puffs of smoke billowed from *The Plague Dolly*. She was closer now. Alfie—and he wasn't proud of this—squealed as a cannonball smashed through the ship's timbers below his feet.

'*Tsh*, I'll bet that's wrecked the first class cabin,' huffed the Professor. 'I'd just dusted, too.'

The deck tilted.

'But what do they *want*?' Alfie gurgled.

'Pirate stuff, I should think,' said the Professor, clinging to the rail. 'Something interesting to put in their next letter to Aunt Lucy, possibly.'

'Load the cannon!' Captain Swag's voice rose above the babble on deck. 'Fire at will! Fire! FIRE! Prepare for battle!'

Putting her knife between her teeth, Derek scrambled into the ship's rigging.

'What should I do?' Flem called after her.

'*Mmmf mmf mmff . . .*' Derek took the knife from her mouth and shouted, 'Don't get killed.'

BOOM

BOOM

With *The Plague Dolly* closing in fast, cannons on the *Jewel of the Breezy Seas* fired back. Alfie covered his ears. Gunpowder smoke billowed around him. As it cleared, he saw that gaping holes had appeared in the pirate ship. Cheers echoed across the deck of the *Jewel of the Breezy Seas*.

That was where the good news ended though.

'They're going to ram us,' screamed Alfie. *The Plague Dolly* was almost on top of them. Tattooed, gold-toothed pirates hung from the rigging. Some had hooks for hands. Fireworks crackled in beards. One or two were wearing dresses, jeering, pointing, and twirling parasols.

'Professor!' yelled Alfie, 'Look out!' Grabbing the old man around the waist, he dragged him to the deck. With a **CRAAACK** and a tearing of timber, *The Plague Dolly* smashed into the *Jewel of the Breezy Seas*. The ship groaned and tilted, sending Alfie and the Professor tumbling across the deck. Arrows *vip-vip-vipped* into the deck around them. Cannon roared again. 'Derek! *Derek!*' Alfie shouted, blinded by thick, evil-smelling gunpowder smoke. Unable to see, he could only hear swords crashing against swords and one of the more elderly passengers asking if the pirate battle was part of the entertainment.

Captain Swag whirled out of the smoke, locked in combat with a pirate who Alfie thought must be Bad Hair O'Hooligan herself. The pirate queen's hair-do did, indeed, look like a nest built by a drunk ostrich. The fireworks woven into her unruly mop probably caused frizziness and split ends, too, Alfie thought.

'What do you call a pirate with three eyes?' squawked Polly on the captain's shoulder.

'Not *now* Polly,' she squealed, ducking a swishing cutlass.

'A Piiirate,' Polly cawed. 'Ha ha ha HA HA HA.'

'Shut *UP*, blast you.' Catching hold of a rope, the captain swung across the deck and planted both boots in Bad Hair O'Hooligan's chest. The pirate queen vanished over the side, screaming.

'Ah-haargh,' Captain Swag yelled. '*Now* we can do jokes. How do you clean a dirty pira—'

'Give her a baaarghth,' squawked her parrot.

'You are the worst parrot in the whole wide

world. You know that, don't you?'

'Stick it up yer eyepatch, Carol,' Polly squawked.

'*Don't* call me Carol,' Captain Swag spat, disappearing back into the smoke.

Alfie stared around in horror. Pirates infested the *Jewel of the Breezy Seas*. The ship was burning now, sails aflame above Alfie's head. Flem staggered backwards, cowering before a pirate wearing an elegant off-the-shoulder number in red velvet that clung to his figure in all the right places.

Derek swung from the rigging. Leaping onto the pirate's back she wrestled him to the deck. The pair of them rolled out of sight in a tumbling whirl of red velvet and dreadlocks and flying punches.

Alfie jumped to his feet. 'Derek!' he yelled. *'DEREK!'*

'Don't you worry about her, you spam-faced ferret-burglar,' said a familiar voice. 'Got you at last, eh? Nowhere to run to on the high seas, is there?'

Saucer-eyed, Alfie gulped as Incontinence Pance and Bernard Stiltskin stepped out of the smoke. Stiltskin, Alfie couldn't help noticing, had replaced his table leg with a wickedly sharp-looking cutlass.

CHAPTER TWENTY-ONE

JOURNEY TO THE BOTTOM OF THE SEA

'You two again,' Alfie groaned, looking from Pance to Stiltskin. 'How did you . . .'

'Followed you across thirty-six worlds, didn't we Bernard?' said Incontinence Pance, snickering. 'Then hitched a lift with Captain O'Hooligan and her crew. Nice bunch of lads. Didn't understand us at first, but using hand gestures—well, it was mostly beating them around the head—we told 'em you was loaded down with treasure. They couldn't wait to get their hands round your scrawny necks after that.'

'Ankles,' said Bernard Stiltskin. 'I seen ankles.'

'Give it a rest, Bernard. You've been going on and on and on about ankles since we left Earth,' Pance grumped. 'Your brain's stuck again. Give it a jiggle and grab these two. Then we can round up the girl and young Nanbiter and be on our way home.'

Stiltskin took a step forward, swinging his shiny new cutlass.

Alfie backed across the tilting deck. 'Now look here,' snapped the Professor, getting to his feet and placing his hands on his hips. 'I've had just about *enough* of you two trailing around after us like a length of toilet paper we accidentally tucked into the back of our trousers. I don't like to complain, but come on. *Really*. I've a good mind to . . .'

'To do *what*, you piddle-faced mattress-fluffer?' snarled Pance. Stiltskin took another step.

'Well . . . I . . . ahh . . . DEREK!' the Professor yelped. *'DEREK!'*

If Derek heard him, she was too busy to answer. Stiltskin took another step across the heaving deck. Again, Alfie backed away. The mast behind stopped him. There was nowhere left to run. He looked up into Stiltskin's brainless eyes, and gulped again.

KERR-ACCCCK

With an ear-splitting crash of timber, a crack appeared in the deck. Alfie's eyes widened as it zigzagged crazily across the width of the *Jewel of the Breezy Seas*, from port to starboard, opening a split between himself and the Professor, and Stiltskin and Pance. Below, seawater boiled into the gap. Stiltskin tottered on the edge, arms windmilling as he tried to keep his balance. Darting forward, Pance grabbed him by the back of his ridiculous puffy shorts and pulled him to safety. 'Ha,' shouted Alfie, across the widening chasm. Breaking into one of Bosun McHearty's best jigs, he yelled, 'Come and get us now, you great ninnies. That sorted *you* out, eh?'

'Ah, Rupert,' said the Professor.

Alfie took no notice. 'And so, we escape once more,' he jeered, hopping from one leg to another and shaking a fist at the two henchmen. 'Foiled again, eh? You've crossed thirty-six worlds only to watch us float away . . .'

'*Sink* away, actually,' the Professor chipped in.

'What?' said Alfie. Stopping his jig, he goggled at

the Professor.

'I was just saying that we appear to be sinking,' said the old man, tugging his moustache. Alfie took this as a bad sign. The Professor only ever tugged his moustache at moments of great emotional stress. The old man paused for a second, then added, 'Never a poodle around to help seafarers in distress when you need one, eh?'

Alfie looked down to see water was swirling around his ankles. He looked up again.

Above, Stiltskin and Pance peered down over the edge of the ship's other half, which was still— miraculously—afloat. 'Looks like you won't be coming back with us after all,' sneered Pance. 'Oh dear, oh dear, what a shame. Still, I expect Sir Willikin will find a way to cope with the disappointment.' As water climbed to Alfie's knees, he waved, adding, 'Goodbye then. Good luck with all your future endeavours: drowning and whatnot. Give our regards to the sharks.'

The ship—or the back half at least—slipped beneath the waves, dragging Alfie down with it. The last thing he saw as the water closed above his

head was Pance grinning and waving. The last thing
he heard was Captain Swag's voice in the distance
yelling 'Abandon ship!'

And then everything was cold and green.

The good ship *Jewel of the Breezy Seas* dragged
Alfie down to the silent depths.

Bubbles streamed from Alfie's mouth. Thrashing at the water, he tried to follow them upwards. The pull of the broken ship beneath him was too strong.

A mermaid swam into view, hair floating prettily around her face. She stared into Alfie's eyes. He reached for her, mouthing the word 'help'.

The mermaid blew him a kiss, and—with a flick of her tail—disappeared.

Let's leave Alfie drowning for a moment and share a few words about mermaids, shall we? Many stories have been told over the years about how they save human princes from drowning. In these stories they always end up swapping their tails for legs, marrying the prince and living happily ever after. In real life this never happens. Ghastly, undersea, half-octopus witches *will* perform a leg transplant operation for a heavy price—usually the mermaid's voice or long, silken hair. That much is true. But it's messy and painful. Half-octopus witches can only use whatever legs they have in stock, too, and decent legs are in short supply beneath the waves.

While *lucky* mermaids might wake up with a pair of bow-legged legs from a drowned sailor, *unlucky* mermaids might find they have swapped their gorgeous, shimmery tail for one grizzled leg and a wooden peg leg. Even for the lucky ones the tale doesn't often end well. The most love-struck prince will quickly cancel the wedding cake after seeing his bride-to-be lurching out of the waves on badly stitched-on legs that once belonged to Seaman 'Hairy' Jake O'Nobbly-Knees. Most mermaids, therefore, avoid saving drowning humans. It all-too-often leads to heartache and athlete's foot.

Back to the story. Our hero is currently in a spot of bother, if you remember.

The last of Alfie's air left his mouth in a string of bubbles. Far above, they popped on the surface, each one whispering a tiny 'help'.

So, this is drowning, he thought to himself. Minutes earlier he had been making beds. Now, his life was flashing before his eyes. From habit, he gave it a review: four stars. It had been a pretty good life. Especially the bits with the Professor in. If maths lessons had been removed it would have been almost perfect. Sadness welled up as he watched visions of his mum drift through his dying brain: the two of them in their old flat, playing board games like *Toast Stabbers!* they'd found in charity shops; the joy on her face when she'd unwrapped the Sole Sensation 6000 foot spa he'd given her for her birthday . . .

A tear leaked from Alfie's eye, adding a single drop to the ten bejillion gallons of salty water drowning him. His mum would never know what had happened to him, unless—somehow—Derek survived and managed to get home.

Derek.

He hadn't said goodbye. Their last conversation had been an argument. Alfie's final tear was for his best friend.

A hand grabbed the back of his t-shirt. Alfie tried kicking his legs, but it was no good—he was too weak. As the lights went out in his brain he smiled. Good old Derek. She had come to save him. She always did.

It was a shame that this time she was too late.

CHAPTER TWENTY-TWO

SHIPWRECKED
ON SOLSTICE

'It's not my first shipwreck, of course. About my twelfth, I think. The first time is always the worst. *My* first shipwreck happened, oh, years ago. 1879, I think it was. I was sailing across the planet of Windlesham, en route to an unmapped continent, when the ship got eaten from beneath by one of those things . . . oh what are they called? Eight legs? Tentacles? Great big googly eyes. Beaky mouth parts . . .'

'An octopus, Professor?'

'No thank you. Too chewy. It's my false teeth, you know. So, as I was saying . . . when you've been

in as many sea disasters as I have you learn to grab
something floaty. Like this lifeboat for example . . .'

'Professor.'

'Yes, Derek old chap?'

'*Shhh*. I think he's coming round.'

'Oh, *marvellous*. Ahoy there, young Rupert. Good
to have you back with us.'

Coughing water, Alfie opened his eyes. Three
heads blotted out the suns above him.

'Still alive then?' said Derek.

Alfie coughed again, turning his head. He was

lying in the bottom of a small boat. So far so good, he told himself. It wasn't a comfortable boat but it was much, *much* better than being tangled in seaweed at the bottom of the ocean. Above him, the heads of Flem, Derek, and the Professor looked down, silhouetted against Solstice's suns. There was something wrong with them but he couldn't quite put his finger on it. 'S-Sorry,' he coughed. 'H-Hope I h-haven't d-disappointed you b-by not being dead.'

'It's all right, I'm used to it,' said Derek. Her face broke into a wide grin. 'Thought we'd lost you for a moment there. Lucky Flem's such a good swimmer.'

Alfie blinked again. 'F-Flem?' he croaked. '*Flem* pulled me out?' Suddenly, he knew what was wrong with the heads above him. Derek's dry dreadlocks whipped her face in the breeze but Flem Nanbiter was soaked. Water dripping off his nose spashed into Alfie's face.

'Yes, *Flem*,' said Derek. 'You remember Flem, don't you? You *must* do. He's that kid you've been giving a *really* hard time since we left Wigless Square.'

Alfie's eyes flicked to Flem's. 'I . . . uh . . . I . . .'

'You're welcome,' said Flem.

'I *was* going to dive in after you, because—you know—that would make *twenty-seven* times I've saved your life,' said Derek. 'But I didn't want to get my hair wet and Flem has years of practice swimming through bogs on Bewayre. *And* he gave you the kiss of life. Well someone had to and we thought you'd prefer Flem to the Professor. Just in case you woke up. We decided the shock of having that moustache on your face might kill you all over again.'

'*Hurrumph,*' hurrumphed the Professor.

'Spurt f'nam f'nam ping b-hark schwing saveloy, Derek,' Alfie muttered.

'You want me to push a carpet into your left nostril?' said Derek. '*Really?* At a time like this? Well, I suppose if it's what you want. I'm not sure we have any carpets but I could use an eel.'

'I *meant*, you're babbling, Derek,' said Alfie, sitting up with a groan. 'Like a Cabbage-Eating Fartpig.'

In reply, Derek threw her arms around him. 'Do *not* die again,' she added. 'Or I'll rip your spleen out and use it as a Frisbee. *Understand?*'

Nodding, Alfie returned the hug and glanced over

Derek's shoulder. Taking a deep breath, he croaked, 'What happened?'

Both *Jewel of the Breezy Seas* and *The Plague Dolly* had vanished. Nothing was left of either ship but drifting smoke and floating wreckage. Groaning sailors, pirates, and cruise passengers clung to barrels or broken ship's timbers. In the distance, Alfie saw Dot and Mavis perched on a wooden chest. Voices drifted across the waves: 'Can you see it? You'll have to dive for it.'

'I am not diving for your false buttock at my age. A shark must've eaten it.'

'But you *know* I can't get comfy without my bum.'

'I *told* you to strap it on tight. Do you listen? No, 'cos you never turn on your ear trumpet. Look, I fished out this jellyfish. We'll chop off the dangly bits and you can use that instead.'

'Both ships sank,' said the Professor, sounding sad. 'Betsy's gone, too, of course. Poor Betsy.'

'Sorry, Professor,' said Alfie.

'I'll never replace her,' the Professor sniffed. 'Still, at least we're all alive, even if we are stranded at sea.'

'Who be stranded at sea?' said a familiar voice.

Alfie turned to see Captain Swag sitting astride the ship's figurehead, using a broken plank to paddle it along. 'Umm . . . is that a trick question?' he replied, looking around at the endless, empty ocean.

'We ain't stranded, bless your landlubbery socks,' said Captain Swag. 'What we have here is your Marooned-on-a-Paradise-Island-Sunshine-Experience.' All part of the service when you come aboard *Jewel of the Breezy Seas*, and at no extra cost. We'll paddle to the nearest desert island then spend a few years in raggedy trousers, growing nice big beards and relaxing on the beach until a passing ship picks us up.'

'You seem very happy, despite—you know—your ship sinking,' Alfie told her.

'It's Polly,' Captain Swag replied, beaming.

'Your parrot?' Alfie glanced at the captain's shoulder. It was empty except for a patch of dried bird droppings.

'Cannonball,' chuckled the captain. 'One second he be there, the next **SQUAWWK**, *pooooof*: cloud of feathers. Best day of me life. I *despised* that parrot.'

'OK. Umm . . . Could we back up a bit and go

over the part where we sit on a desert island growing beards for years,' said Alfie.

'Unless you want to *row* to the Isle of Sheds,' said Captain Swag, pointing. 'It's about a hundred miles that way.'

Derek was already reaching for the oars.

'Good luck to ye then.' Captain Swag waved her hat while the little boat skidded away across the waves. 'We thank you for travelling with Captain Swag's Luxury Cruises. Please think of us when planning your next island-hopping, bloody pirate battle, marooned-on-a-desert-island voyage.'

For a few minutes there was silence except for the rhythmic splashes of oars. All four questers stared ahead at the horizon, where suns were setting and Catsic the Henge—hopefully—awaited them. After a while, Flem said, 'You were right. The sky is *exactly* the same colour as ham.'

CHAPTER TWENTY-THREE
FLOATING SEWAGE

'Help! Save us!'

Derek stopped rowing. Shading his eyes, Alfie looked around, spotting nothing but broken planks, waterlogged bingo cards, and Dot's gently bobbing false buttock.

'Help!' the pitiful voice cried again. 'Help us kind strangers, afore we drown to death.'

The boat bumped against something hard.

'Oww,' said the same voice. 'Watch where you're going you turnip-headed donkey nudger.'

Alfie peered over the side of the boat. 'Hello again, Pance,' he said. 'Help you with something?'

'Oh, it's *you*,' said Incontinence Pance, treading

water while scowling up. 'Help! Help us you dribbling bag of otter snot. We're drowning, ain't we Bernard?'

'Ankles,' said Bernard Stiltskin.

'Well, good luck with that,' Alfie replied. 'Give my regards to the sharks. Derek, let's go.'

'Wait,' yelped Flem Nanbiter. 'We can't just leave them to die.'

'Why not? They left *me* to die.'

'But . . . but . . .' Flem stammered.

'Flem just saved your life,' Derek said, raising an eyebrow. 'I mean, all right, I suppose I would have dived in if I had to, but I think that gives him a say. Don't you?'

'No, I don't think it does.' Alfie huffed. 'Stiltskin and Pance laughed and pointed while I *drowned*.'

Derek shrugged, and turned to Flem. 'The twonk makes a good point,' she said, lifting an oar. 'If you like I could give them both a bonk on the head. It'd be a quick, boring death.'

'Make up yer minds,' gargled Pance, spitting water. 'We *are* actually drowning here.'

'Anyway,' continued Alfie, ignoring him. 'It's for

the best. These two won't be voting for anything from inside a shark. All we have to do is grab Catsic and the quest's over. It doesn't even matter if Flem votes for his dad. We'll still have four votes against three so I can stop pretending to like him . . .' Realizing what he'd just said, Alfie's voice trailed off.

'Ahh, Rupert,' said the Professor. 'That was *not* well done. It reminds me of an old saying: "What price a man's tonsils if all around him is dust". No wait, that's not right, it goes "What price . . ."'

No one paid much attention. All eyes were fixed on Flem, who had taken a sharp breath. 'So that's why you were making faces,' he hissed. 'I *knew* you weren't pleased to see me.'

'You're not part of this quest,' Alfie growled back. 'I never wanted you along.'

'Ankles,' groaned Bernard Stiltskin.

'Why does he keep wittering on about ankles?' Alfie snapped, glancing down at the heads in the water.

'There's something nibbling at them,' said Pance, desperation in his voice. 'Look, I see this is awkward. Laughing while you drownded? Well, that was naughty—you've got me there, ha ha. When you *really* think about it, it's quite funny though, isn't it? I mean, the sharks are eating the other foot now, eh?'

Seeing no one laughing, Pance continued. 'No sense of humour, eh? Right you are. But if you're *going* to save us could you get on with it?'

Alfie glared at Flem. Flem glared back at him. 'I know you want to save your Unusual Travel Agency,' he said. 'Are you willing to let people *die* for it?'

'They watched me . . . oh, *all right.*'

With only a few near-capsizes, Stiltskin and Pance were dragged aboard. Both sat shivering in the stern while Derek tied their hands.

'Caught you in the middle of a tiff, did we?' said Pance, his magnified eye darting from Alfie to Flem. The two boys were still glaring at each other. 'Well, if you wants my advice . . .'

'No one wants your advice,' Alfie told him, taking the oars.

He rowed on, anger fading while he pulled the boat onwards into starry darkness. It had been a busy day and soon Flem and Derek were slumped against each other, snoring. After an hour or so Pance and Stiltskin did the same. When he was sure they were asleep Alfie said, quietly, 'Professor, is Derek right? Have I been a bit of a twonk? About Flem, I mean.'

The Professor took a while to answer. 'Ahh,' he said, eventually. 'I wondered when you'd work it out. Yes, Rupert. You *have* been a bit of a spoon.'

'How bad?'

'Quite bad, actually. The boy's not to blame for his dad, you know. He actually seems a decent enough young fellow. Young Derek seems to think so, and she's usually quite sensible when she isn't trying to twist someone's head off.'

'He's still going to vote with his dad, you know. He's . . . he's . . . too weak. Is weak the word I'm looking for?'

'*Broken* would be better, Rupert,' the Professor told him, his voice sad in the darkness. 'His father's broken his spirit. He's had a difficult life, I think.'

'I . . . uh . . . yes. Growing up on Bewayre with Sir Willikin for a dad must have been awful. I see that. I guess I *was* a little harsh.' Alfie suddenly felt very small.

'That's what I like about you,' the Professor continued. 'You're always ready to admit when you've made a mistake. I've met too many people who'd rather be boiled alive in sick than admit they weren't right about everything. Sir Willikin for one.'

'What should I do?' Alfie asked.

'Oh, you'll put things right,' said the Professor, his voice brighter. 'It's what you do, isn't it? For now—and I mean *right* now—what you should do is row towards that island over there. It's my bladder, you know.'

Alfie changed course. A few minutes later, the boat ran aground on a hump of sand in the middle of the ocean. A single palm tree sprouted from the centre. While the Professor went to stand behind it, Alfie poked Flem's shoulder. 'Look,' he whispered. 'I know it's not much, but for what it's worth, I'm sorry.'

'It's a start.' Flem yawned, smiled, and closed his eyes again.

CHAPTER TWENTY-FOUR

WHAT WOULD SIR WILLIKIN DO?

OOOOH, WHEN YOU'RE ALWAYS AWARE OF THE LICE IN YOUR HAIR, YOU'RE A SAILOR! WHEN YOU'VE GOT THE SCUR-VEE, 'COS THERE'S NO VITAMIN C, YOU'RE A SAILOR! AND YOU LOOK TWICE YOUR AGE 'COS OF ALL THE SUN DAM-AGE, YOU'RE A SAILOR! YOU'VE GOT A HOOK HAND, ONE LEG AND ONE EYE AND YOU'RE SOON GONNA DIE IT'S A SAILOR'S LIFE FOR MEEEEE!

Everyone on the lifeboat stopped singing and

looked at each other.

'This is a really depressing sea shanty,' said Derek.

'Yeah,' Alfie agreed. 'It really is. Shall we play I-Spy, instead?'

I-Spy wasn't a success either. Once the questers had spied 'sea', 'sky', 'sea monster', and 'Incontinence Pance', the game was pretty much over. Silence fell again. Taking turns at the oars, the tired questers pulled the boat on over glassy, clear water, hour after hour.

Alfie tried passing the time by naming and reviewing the islands they stopped at.

DISCOVERING . . . TOILET-BREAK ISLAND NUMBER THIRTY-SIX

Featuring conveniently thick bushes with velvet soft leaves, this is a five-star stop for lost seafarers looking for that little bit of luxury. Visitors will, yet again, appreciate the chance to complete their business in the fresh air, and the island's population of monkeys are a great audience who applaud loudly while throwing bananas.

'I learned some songs from the natives on Bewayre,' said Flem on the third sun-blistered day. 'They're full of loneliness and suffering but hopeful for a brighter tomorrow. Sort of heartbreaking, really. Does anyone want to hear one?'

'That depends,' said Alfie. 'Do the Bewayrians sing of wiping snot on each other?'

Flem thought about it. 'Yes,' he said, eventually. 'Yes they do.'

'Then despite the fact that I am trying to be properly nice to you I'm going to pass,' Alfie told him.

'Anyone for a fun and exciting game of head-butt?' asked Derek, brightly. 'It's a traditional Children-of-Skingrath game for ages four to ninety-four.'

'*No*,' said everyone on the boat at the same time.

Silence fell again, the dip-dip-dipping of the oars the only sound.

'I could tell stories of my adventures in the UCC,' said the Professor. 'That might help pass the time.'

'Please, not stories *again*,' Pance yelped. 'If he's going to start *stories* again, just throw us to the sharks. By the way, we've been out here for days now. We'd go a lot quicker if you let Bernard take the oars. He's a strong lad, ain't you, Bernard?'

'Oars,' said Stiltskin, nodding.

'Oh right. So we untie him and give him a pair of blunt instruments.' Alfie sighed. 'That sounds like it would turn out well.'

'Fair point,' said Stiltskin.

'He knows what you're doing, you know,' Pance replied, leaning forward and staring into Alfie's face through his broken glasses. 'Sir Willikin, I mean. He's a clever one. Cleverer than you lot anyway. Seeing as you saved me and Bernard's lives, I'll give you this advice as a favour: stay here. It's a nice enough planet. You could do worse. Oh, you might find the old duffer you're looking for but then what, eh? Sir Willikin will just outsmart you again. Best for you if you stay here. Let us go and we'll tell Sir W you all drownded. Everyone's happy. Deal?'

'No,' said Alfie.

'Then you're a fool,' said Pance. Leaning back

against Stiltskin, he closed his massive eye. 'No *stories*,' he added.

The overcrowded boat skimmed on, carrying its ragged, sunburned occupants towards the Isle of Sheds. Alfie frowned. Pance had a point. Beyond finding Catsic the Henge, he hadn't thought about what came next. If Pance was telling the truth Sir Willikin would be making plans for their return.

But what plans? *What* might Sir Willikin do?

What would *he* do, if he were Sir Willikin, Alfie wondered.

Before his brain could answer, Derek stood in the prow of the boat, shouting, 'Land! We're here. We're *finally* here. *Look.*'

Every head in the boat turned to look at the Isle of Sheds.

DISCOVERING . . . THE ISLE OF SHEDS

Imagine a shed. Multiply it by about forty thousand into a heaped and jumbled city of sheds. Make some of your sheds much, much bigger than your average shed, and others quite dinky. Imagine tall sheds—great, towering ones that scratch the sky yet are still obviously sheds with their rickety slatted wooden walls and green roofs. Make others low and squat, sprawling along the ground like aircraft hangars with windows that look like they're about to fall out. Add sheds onto sheds, so that many of your sheds are sprouting sheds from their upper sheds, and some of *those* sheds have still smaller shed extensions. After all that, add still more sheds. Put sheds out at sea, standing on stilts, and one or two peculiar, experimental flying sheds in the sky above, moored to other sheds by long ropes and gently circling. When you've imagined all that you'll still have only the vaguest idea of how many sheds had been built on the Isle of Sheds.

In short: if you're a shed fan, this is the place to be.

'He must have a *lot* of gardening tools and old pots of paint,' Alfie murmured

'Just think how many spiders there must be,' added the Professor staring up at the immense shedopolis.

'This Catsic *really* likes sheds,' Derek added.

'Are we here? Is this the Isle of Sheds?' asked Flem. Ahead, lay a small jetty. Beside it a man wearing long white robes was busy building a shed. His beard trailed across the ground and into the water.

'Let's ask *him*,' Alfie continued. Cupping his hands around his mouth, he shouted, 'Excuse me. Is this the Isle of Sheds?'

The man turned. Spitting nails, he snapped, 'What sort of cack-brained question is that, Alfie Fleet? You're supposed to be *clever*. Is this the Isle of flippin' Sheds? Take a look around. See all these sheds? What do *you* think?'

'I'm guessing it *is* the Isle of Sheds,' Alfie replied. 'Hang on . . . how do you know my name?'

CHAPTER TWENTY-FIVE
SURPRISE #1

'You're late,' said the man, by way of an answer to Alfie's question. 'Thought I'd put up a quick shed while I waited. You can never have too many sheds. That's what I say.' Stepping back he looked at his new shed proudly.

'Are you sure about that?' asked Alfie. 'I'd have thought two sheds was about as many sheds as anyone would ever need. Three, maximum.'

'Rubbish,' said the man. 'I need extra space for those boxes of little metal widgets that might come in handy one day. Come on then, get out of the boat. Let's have a look at you.'

The lifeboat's prow nudged the jetty. Grabbing a rope, Alfie jumped out and tied it safely, then turned back to the old man. Behind his beard, which did indeed look like a wispy ghost was clinging to his face, his skin was lined and creased like a shirt balled up at the bottom of the wash basket. A few lonely white hairs sprang from his pink, spotted scalp as if trying to decide whether to jump. From beneath sheepy eyebrows, twinkling blue eyes watched Alfie's companions clamber onto the jetty.

'Goodness,' said the Professor, before Alfie

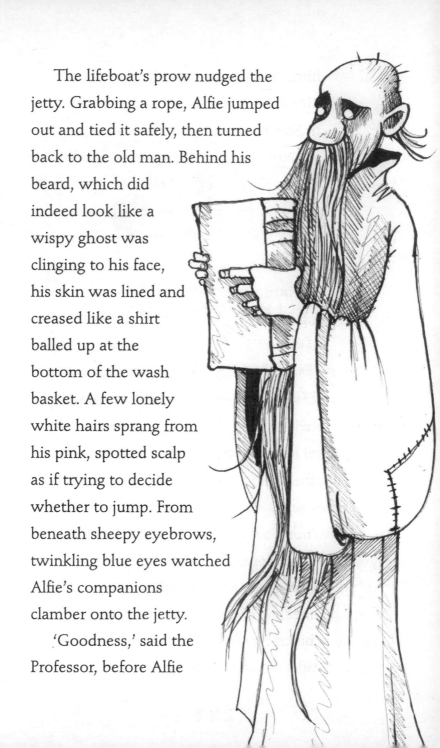

could stop him. 'You're a proper elderly old muffin, aren't you? Reminds me of the time I met the Very Ancient Soothsayer of Nubbin. He was quite wrinkled, too. Not as wrinkled as you, of course, but even so, quite wrinkled. Had to wash his face with a little rag on the end of a twig. Only way he could get into all the wrinkles and crevices, you see?'

'Met the Soothsayer of Nubbin, did you, you cheeky young whippersnapper?' the old man snorted. 'That's nothing. *I've* met Death.'

'Death?' said the Professor, blinking in confusion. '*The* Death? The Slim Reaper? Carries around a big potato peeler?'

'The *Grim Reaper*,' Alfie murmured.

'No, it's the *Slim* Reaper,' the Professor insisted. 'Skinny, you see? Very bony chap.'

'And it's not a potato peeler it's a . . . actually, you know what? Forget it.' Alfie turned back to Catsic. 'You've met Death?' he said, impressed. 'What's he like?'

'*She* is a bit cranky in the mornings,' said Catsic, peering at Alfie. 'So, you're finally here, eh? Hmm, pretty much what I was expecting. Knees a bit strange but you can't have everything, I suppose.'

Deciding to let that pass, Alfie said, 'You must be Catsic the Henge.'

'In the baggy old flesh,' said Catsic the Henge. 'And you must be the boy whose destiny is to lead the universe into a new age of peace and harmony.'

Let's take a break there. From time to time across the universe, destiny will give someone a prod: magical young people with odd birthmarks who rise from mucking out pigs to become king/queen; snail creatures whose destiny it is to follow a magical trail of slime and defeat the wicked slugwitch in epic feeler-to-feeler combat. That sort of thing. Destiny's children react to the news that they have been touched by greatness in very different ways. Some fall to their knees, sobbing as they realize the heavy responsibility of their fate. Others pour shockfoam from their armpit gills or spin worried circles on their cabbage leaf. Let's see how Alfie reacts to the news that he, and he alone, has been selected to decide the future of the universe, shall we?

'Yeah, right. Whatevs.' he sighed, groaning quietly to himself. After everything they had been through, Catsic the Henge was clearly barmy as a box of frogs.

'And you can wipe that look off your face,' said Catsic. 'I may be wrinkly, but I'm not bonkers thankyousoverymuch.'

'Mmm hmm,' said Alfie, raising an eyebrow.

'No *really*,' snapped Catsic, crossing his arms. 'I've checked, you know. Consulted the Holy Face of Nipsy, The Grand High Seeress at the Intergalactic Fork, the Coughing Priests at the Temple of Cataar, the Know-it-All Space Crystal of Sponge, the Mystic Serpent of Nerwong Nerwong Plinky-Plonk . . . They all agree it's your destiny.'

'The Mystic Serpent of Nerwong Nerwong Plinky-Plonk?' said Alfie. 'We thought that was a sock with buttons sewn on for eyes.'

'The Mystic Serpent is one of the most intelligent beings in the known universe,' said Catsic. 'She can see the future in infinite dimensions.'

'Oh good. So not a sock with buttons sewn on. That's saved us a trip, eh Rupert?' said the Professor.

'Yeah, I'll cross it off the to-do list now, while I remember,' Alfie replied, rummaging in his rucksack for the Unusual Travel Agency's half-finished to-do list.

'Look,' said Catsic. 'Will you put that away and *listen*. I'm trying to tell you that *you* . . . are . . . destined . . . to . . . lead . . .'

'Ah-*hem*, if I may interrupt for a moment,' the Professor interrupted. 'Rupert, I think the rickety old fellow is trying to tell you that you, Rupert, are destined to lead the universe into a new age of peace and harmony.' Looking pleased with himself, he smiled around at everyone. 'Well done,' he added, though it wasn't clear whether he was talking to himself or Alfie.

'So, what you're saying, is that I'm destined to lead the universe into a new age of peace and harmony,' Alfie repeated.

'Yes, that's exactly what I'm saying.'

'Nifty,' said Alfie. 'You're sure though? I mean, you've only just met me so you're not to know, but—as Derek and Flem here will tell you—I'm basically a bit of a twonk.'

'Yes, I can see that,' said Catsic. 'Probably wouldn't have been my first choice. But what can you do? Can't argue with destiny.'

'So . . . so, just to be clear . . . when it comes right down to it . . . nitty gritty and all that . . . what you're saying is that—despite being a bit of a twonk—I'm some sort of Chosen One?'

'I *suppose* you could put it like that,' said Catsic. 'Also you could say you're just some kid with weird knees who happens to be in the right place at the right time to change the course of universal history.'

'No . . . no. I'll stick with Chosen One, if that's all right.'

Catsic shrugged. 'No skin off my nose,' he said. 'Might give people the idea that you're a twonk though.'

Alfie wasn't listening. 'Hey, Derek,' he said, nudging her. 'Did you hear that? I'm the *Chosen One*!'

Derek rolled her eyes.

'Of all the boys in all the universe only one can lead humanity to its ultimate destiny,' Alfie continued, raising his eyes to the heavens. 'That's me, by the way. Just in case you didn't get that: the *Chosen* One.'

Derek looked up at the Professor with pleading eyes. 'Can I kill him *now?*' she asked.

'I'm ... ah ... not entirely sure how destiny works, Derek old chap,' said the Professor, patting her shoulder. 'If this crumbly old geezer is correct, then I should think there would be quite a high risk. Killing young Rupert means he won't achieve his destiny, you see? So you'd probably plunge the entire universe into an age of darkness and misery.'

'Worth it,' said Derek, grumpily.

'Chosen One,' Alfie repeated.

'Kid with strange knees is what I heard,' said Derek.

'That's that all sorted then,' said Catsic the Henge. 'I suppose you'd all better come in.'

'Is there a magic sword that comes with the job?' Alfie asked, his heart leaping.

'Like *you* could use a magic sword,' Derek snorted. 'What are you gonna do with it? Cut sandwiches?'

'And maybe a cape,' Alfie murmured.

'Of course there's no magic sword, *or* a cape, you little twerp,' said Catsic. 'I must say, your friend here has the right idea. I may kill you myself before the end of the day.'

SURPRISE #2

PRESIDENT NO. 328
Catsic the Henge (c.502–467 BCE)

Little is known for certain about the Unusual Cartography Club's most famous historical president although it is said that his tribe voted him Person Most Likely to Succeed after he grew his first beard at age six. Today, he is remembered for updating the UCC's map-making methods, for example telling members to make charts that looked at least a little bit like the lands they were supposed to be mapping rather than making stuff up then adding extra sea monsters.

From Presidents of the Ancient and Unusual Cartography Club, Volume I

A grin plastered to his face, Alfie mumbled the words 'Chosen One' to himself while his feet followed Catsic of their own accord. The Professor walked behind, with Derek and Flem at the back, poking the still-tied Stiltskin and Pance forwards. Too busy wondering if his mum might make him a cape, Alfie barely noticed as they were led through door after door covered in flaking green paint.

This was a shame, as the interior of the shed city was really something. One shed led into another, from small, cramped shed into football pitch sized shed to long, corridor-type shed, forming a maze of endless sheds. Groaning, dusty shelves contained millions—*billions*—of books, jammed onto shelves in no particular order.

It's worth mentioning that, in fact, Catsic the Henge owned a copy of every book ever written. What he *didn't* have was any kind of filing system, so his signed copy of *The Universe: A User's Guide* by the High Priest Kippy Blowhole of planet Podensack had been stuffed between copies of *Sally's First Potato* and *The Art of Wearing Trousers*.

Elsewhere were heaped piles of maps, some drawn with burned twigs on tree bark, others in faded ink on animal skins. Heaps of souvenirs, artworks, and gadgets from a multitude of worlds spilled from cobwebbed boxes. As might be expected there were—here and there—a few tins of old paint that had dried up long ago, boxes of rusty screws and bits of wood in not-very-useful lengths. There were workbenches, too. Clearly, Catsic liked to tinker. They were littered with half-finished projects: a chair with one wing sprouting from a leg, suits of armour spilling cogs and levers from

their guts, and what looked like a toasted sandwich maker. The questers also passed three full-size circles, two half-built and one of glimmering silver, which was spinning lazily.

Alfie took no notice whatsoever. Flem, on the other hand, looked around in awe, gasping occasionally. 'Don't touch that,' shouted Catsic when he stopped and lifted a metal bowler hat studded with blinking lightbulbs.

'Oh,' said Flem, caught in the act of lowering it onto his head. 'What? Why? What does it do?'

'It expands the mind,' snapped Catsic. 'You will instantly become one with all creation, understanding all that has been and all that will ever be.'

'Oh, and that's bad, is it?' asked Flem.

'Not particularly, but it's very boring,' said Catsic. 'I once sat all the way through. It starts off all right—the Big Bang's quite entertaining—but the final Great Cold Extinction? Meh. A let-down, to be honest. And the stuff in the middle goes on and on.'

The Professor nudged Alfie. 'Not too sure about this Matchstick fellow, Rupert,' he whispered. 'Tells a lot of silly stories.'

'Uh,' said the Chosen One. 'What?'

Out loud, the Professor said, 'Remarkable place you have here, Matchstick old chap. Keeping up your interests in the autumn years of your life, eh? That's the way. You old folk need your hobbies, or your brains turn to porridge. Have you thought about growing cucumbers?'

Catsic stopped, and turned. 'Don't give me any of your lip, Bowell-Mouvemont,' he snapped. 'I am *not* happy with you.'

The Professor reddened. 'I say! What have *I* done?'

'Destiny gave you *one* job,' Catsic sniffed. 'You were *supposed* to keep the UCC ticking along until Alfie's Unusual Travel Agency opened. And what happened? You *fluffed* it. Let Sir Willikin Nanbiter back in.'

'Of all the nerve . . .' the Professor spluttered.

'It wasn't *his* fault,' Alfie cut in. 'We didn't know what was supposed to happen. It's not as if destiny gave us any hints.'

Catsic goggled at him. 'You . . . you . . . Didn't give you any *hints?*' he gurgled. 'You discover a universe-travelling stone circle, pootle off to other worlds, meet Hunter-Of-The-Vicious-Spiny-Dereko-Beast, and start the first intergalactic travel agency in thousands of years. That's not enough of a *hint* for you?' He shook his head in wonder. 'What does destiny have to *do*? Slap you around the face, shouting "Oi, this is your destiny"?'

'Hey,' Derek squawked. 'I'm not part of his stupid destiny. Leave me out of it.'

'Don't be ridiculous,' Catsic said, tutting. 'You're

Alfie's protector, destined since the dawn of time itself to keep him alive while he completes his task. *Excellent* work, by the way. It can't have been easy, what with destiny-boy being such a prannet.'

'True,' said Derek, nodding. 'I'm glad you see that. Not many people do.'

'Bravo. You're doing a much better job than *some* people.' Catsic shot the Professor a dark look. '*You*,' he said, pointing at Flem. '*Your* destiny lies along a different path.'

Flem gulped. '*I* have a destiny, too?' he said. 'What is it?'

'No time for that now,' Catsic snapped, marching off again. 'Stuff to do. Hurry along. Follow me.'

The little group set off again, trailing after Catsic and passing through shed after wonder-stuffed shed.

'Do we have a destiny?' Pance asked, eventually. 'Me and Bernard, I mean.'

Catsic stopped. Turning, he said, 'What do *you* think? Hmm?'

'Are we the misunderstood but plucky heroes who deliver this mouldy little specimen to his stupid destiny?' asked Pance, sounding hopeful.

'No,' said Catsic.

'Loveable villains?'

'Ha,' said Catsic. '*Loveable*, he says! Nope.'

'What then?'

Catsic jabbed Pance in the chest with a twiggy finger. 'When books are written about Alfie Fleet,' he said. 'You, Incontinence Pance, and your mush-brain friend whose name I can't be bothered to remember, will be spackles of fly poo in the footnotes at the end. Not the villains but the villain's idiot assistants who even the villain secretly hates. The cowpats on a nice walk that history scrapes off its boots and forgets. Got it?'

'Oh,' said Pance. 'I was hoping at least we'd be the maggot-hearted rogues everyone loves to hate.'

'No,' said Catsic. 'You'd really have to raise your game and put in serious amounts of extra work to become the maggot-hearted rogues everyone loves to hate.'

'Cowpats,' mumbled Bernard Stiltskin, while Catsic strode on towards yet another door.

'Wait,' yelped Alfie, hurrying to catch up. 'People are going to write *books* about me?'

Catsic sighed.

'*Alfie Fleet: Champion of the Universe* would be a good title,' said Alfie, ignoring the fact that Catsic was ignoring him. 'Or just *The Chosen One*. Yes, I like that. The cover could have a picture of me looking into the distance, against a background of swirling galaxies. I'd be looking sort-of serious but with a slight smile that says, "Hey, I may be the saviour of the universe but deep down I'm still a normal kind of—"'

'And here we are,' Catsic interrupted, throwing open yet another shed door.

Alfie stepped through the door. Up until that point he'd been having a pretty weird day. Now, it got exactly fifteen and a half times weirder. '*Gah*,' he croaked. 'Wh . . . wh . . .'

'Just a little something I threw together,' said Catsic, smirking. 'Snazzy, huh?'

'Cripes,' croaked the Professor.

'Wowzers,' said Derek. '*Sparkly.*'

'It's *beautiful*,' whispered Flem.

'Thank you,' said Catsic. 'It wasn't easy finding the stones. They have to be flawless, you see. Took me *ages* to build, but it can send you anywhere in the universe. Of course, that comes as standard with any circle. But it also has a number of extra features, such as a pinpoint guidance system and automatic planet detection. And—if I do say so myself—it provides a comfortable ride leaving you refreshed at the end of your journey. There's also a dimension-hopping gizmo, plus a great sound system and a cup-holder. Yes, yes, I'm really quite proud of it. What do *you* think, you weird-kneed Saviour of the Universe?'

Alfie opened his mouth, but no words came out. He was no longer the Chosen One, he was a boy gazing in wonder at the most magnificent object he had ever clapped eyes upon. Sunlight streamed through skylights above, blazing into white fire on the circle. Just looking at it, he could tell it was *perfect*. It was the circle other circles could only dream of becoming. At least six times bigger than Stonehenge, the Wigless Square stone circle would have looked like a ring of pebbles next to it. As his eyes adjusted to the light, Alfie saw tiny planets floating in the dazzle. Hundreds of them. Thousands. Star systems. Entire *galaxies*. Silently, he put his hand up to touch a ping-pong ball sized world as it drifted past his nose. His hand went straight through. Finally, he managed to speak. 'Is

it . . . ? Are those . . . ? Is it made of . . . ?'

'*Diamonds*,' said Catsic, sounding just a little bit pleased with himself. 'Yes, Alfie. This is the universe's first and only *diamond* circle.'

CHAPTER TWENTY-SEVEN
A WHOLE NEW WORLD

'Now,' said Catsic, pulling a remote control from his pocket, 'The Chosen One and I are going to have a chat in private. The rest of you wait here. Don't *touch* anything,' he added, giving the Professor a sharp look. 'I know what you young people are like, Pewsley my boy. Naughty fingers getting into everything.'

'Umm . . . ahh . . . right. I mean . . . yes mummy,' spluttered the Professor.

'For crying out loud,' Catsic muttered to himself while pressing buttons. The diamond circle spun, sending galaxies whirling around the room like a glitter ball at a disco. When it stopped, an almost transparent planet hung in the air directly above the colossal circle, much bigger than the small worlds passing Alfie's nose. Looking up at it he could see strange continents, mountains, and weather systems on the surface. 'Ahh yes, that's another feature,' said Catsic. 'You can see where you're going before you get there. Brilliant, eh? Anyhoo, come along, you universe-saving young freak.' Tossing his beard over his shoulder, he disappeared between two blinding diamond pillars.

Taking a deep breath, Alfie followed.

The journey lasted the blink of an eye, but an eye-blink that had been stretched out for relaxing, refreshing hours. Soft white light surrounded him. Soothing harp music played, making Alfie feel like he was in heaven, or a really posh elevator. By the time he stepped out, he felt lemon-fresh and bouncy. 'That was nice,' he said, gazing around at a landscape that would score only one or two on the Fleet Unusuality Scale. In fact, the planet he was standing on was a lot like Earth, if Earth had had a spring clean. There were no roads or houses or shops selling stuff no one really needed. No billboards shouting advertisements. No car fumes, sirens going off, or people arguing. Bee-like things buzzed quietly. Catsic the Henge sat beneath a tree loaded with fruit and was munching what looked like a plum.'

From habit, Alfie pulled a New Planet Information Sheet from his rucksack. 'Where are we? What planet *is* this?' he asked.

'Classic Class Eight planet,' Catsic mumbled through a mouthful of fruit. 'Earth-type. Standard gravity, low *magical* gravity. Very common. Nothing special. But all right if you like your planets on the dull side.'

'I meant, what's it *called?*' said Alfie, pencil poised over the paper.

'It doesn't have a name yet,' said Catsic the Henge, wiping juice from his beard and patting the ground next to him. While Alfie sat, he continued, 'There's no intelligent life here, unless you count the bees. *They* call it "Bzzz" I believe. You can give it a proper name if you like.'

Alfie blinked, feeling the pressure of naming an

entire *planet*. The only thing he'd ever named before was the class hamster, Mister Tiddles. He ummed, he ahhed, sucking the end of his pencil.

'Don't take all day about it. Universe to save and all that.'

Alfie wrote down the first thing that came into his head.

'You're calling it Clean Pants,' said Catsic, leaning over his shoulder as he scribbled. 'Charming.'

'I know, it's a stupid name,' said Alfie, looking in his rucksack for an eraser. 'But I should've brought more than one extra pair with me. I've been thinking about clean pants a *lot* for the last couple of weeks. Look, just give me a second and I'll come up with something else. How about Derekonia? Or . . .'

Catsic waved a hand. 'No one *cares*, you daft wazzock. No, stop that. If I can finally have your full attention we have matters to discuss.'

As a side note, many UCC explorers had discovered that naming a world is more difficult than you might think. You need something catchy and easy-to-remember but weighty and majestic: a name like Uranus, for example.

THE UCC'S TOP TEN MOST STUPID NAMES EVER GIVEN TO A NEW WORLD

1. World of Bagfolk
2. 3,000 Farts
3. Planet-With-a-Spindly-One-Legged-Thing
4. Cauliflowers Ahoy!
5. Hufty Hufty Hufty
6. Maureen
7. Exploding Nancy
8. Whiffyhole
9. Noddy Pudding
10. Let's-Poop-Cheerfully

Alfie put his clipboard away. 'Why are we here?' he asked, helping himself to a low-hanging plum.

Catsic put his hands behind his head and leaned back against the tree, eyes closing in the warm sunshine. 'We are here, Alfie Fleet, because you need to understand the importance of your fate,' he said. 'In a way, it's a sort of test, too.'

'Oh I get it,' Alfie said. 'It's a Chosen One thing, right? Chosen Ones are *always* tested. I've read books. What do I have to do? Muck out the pigs?'

'Has anyone ever told you that you're an odd boy?' asked Catsic, opening one eye to peer at him.

Alfie nodded. 'Derek does. About three times a day. Flem, too, now. Oh, and my mum. To be honest, it's only the Professor who doesn't. Compared to himself, I guess I look fairly normal.'

Now they were alone, the Stone Age president of the UCC seemed less cranky. Deciding it was OK to relax, Alfie said, 'May I ask a question, Mr the Henge?'

'Catsic will do. Fire away.'

'If you know so much, Catsic, and my destiny is so important, and you have this *amazing* diamond circle, why didn't you come and give us a hand in the first place?' asked Alfie, allowing himself to sound a little cheesed off. 'When Nanbiter first showed up, I mean. It would have saved us a long, pirate-infested journey. *And* the Professor lost his moped. He was very attached to Betsy.'

'The answer to your question is simple,' said Catsic, crossing his eyes to look at a butterfly that had landed on his nose. 'The Mystical Serpent of Nerwong Nerwong Plinky-Plonk—and she understands this kind of thing much better than me—says the universe finds a way to make use of people. Flemming Nanbiter was never supposed to arrive on Earth, but once he did fate wove him into the fabric of your destiny, and mine, too, as a matter of fact. Something I'm quite pleased about. There was some last minute rejigging of the infinite strands of fate and the result was that you, Flem, and Derek needed to take a trip together. Get to know each other.'

'But I *hated* him for most of the trip.'

'And now?' said the old man.

'Well, I guess he's all right,' Alfie admitted. 'He saved my life, and—y'know—totally gets props for that.'

'Mmm,' said Catsic, watching the butterfly flutter away.

'Why did I need to get to know him?'

'You'll be working closely together in future,' Catsic told him. 'But that's for later. We have other things to talk about. Has that little squirt Bowell-Mouvemont told you the history of stone circles?'

Alfie nodded. 'They were invented by a man called Partley Mildew on planet Wip-Bop-a-Looma, starting a craze for interstellar tourism.'

'He did *something* right then,' said Catsic, plucking another plum. 'Yes. A craze that came to an end thousands of years ago. There were once great circle hubs, you know, sending people on their holidays to planets in every corner of the universe.'

'We found one on Outlandish,' said Alfie, nodding again.

'Then you discovered a historical treasure beyond price.'

'Yeah. I sort of blew it up.' Alfie blushed.

Catsic rolled his eyes. 'As I was saying, there were circles on *thousands* of planets. The universe was an interesting place to be back in those days. It was a great Age of Exploration.'

'I *know* all this,' Alfie told him. 'I *am* Vice-

President of the Unusual Travel Agency. After a while people got bored and stopped hopping from planet to planet. The Professor told me.'

'He didn't tell you everything because he doesn't *know* everything,' Catsic replied. 'There used to be societies on thousands of planets, sort of a cross between the Unusual Cartography Club and the Unusual Travel Agency. They controlled the circles, discovered and mapped new worlds, and—most importantly—sent folk on holiday. But, humans being humans, people got greedy. The cost of travel went up. Meanwhile, the societies grew jealous of their secrets. The more people who knew how to build stone circles, the more competition there was and the less money they could make. They began guarding their knowledge closely.'

'They were run by people like Sir Willikin.'

Catsic nodded. '*Exactly*. It was a disaster. Only a chosen few were allowed to join the clubs. Over centuries, the number of people who knew how to build a circle dwindled. Meanwhile—as your Professor told you—everyone else slowly forgot the power of stone circles. They couldn't afford to use them so they stopped thinking about them. After a couple of thousand years hardly any universe-travelling societies were left. By the time you arrived in Wigless Square the Unusual Cartography Club was the *only* one remaining across the entire universe. Did you know that?'

Alfie shook his head.

'That's why it was so important for the Bowell-Mouvemont boy to keep it safe. Even there though, the original purpose of the stone circles was forgotten.' Catsic snorted. 'Finding and mapping new worlds was only *part* of the mission! They were *always* supposed to be travel agencies too.'

'And that's where I come in,' said Alfie, who was beginning to understand what the universe had planned for him.

'Yes. Your Universal Travel Agency will change *everything*,' Catsic replied. 'Once again humans will travel the universe. The UTA will open branches across Earth first and then across all of space. Civilizations that have been adrift from each other for tens of thousands of years will discover they have cousins on other planets. *New* planets will be populated. People and aliens everywhere will hold hands or feelers or tentacles or whatever in a great circle of friendship. Sentimental nonsense if you ask me but the universe *loves* that kind of thing. Anyway, you see where I'm going with this—your task is to bring about the next great age of peace, adventure, and reasonably priced tourism.'

'And all I have to do is what I was going to do anyway,' said Alfie, disappointed. 'There's nothing really special about me, after all.' He paused, shrugged, and—because he was basically a level-headed kind of boy—added, 'Oh well.'

Catsic had drifted off into a snooze. Alfie looked around at the peaceful but badly named world of Clean Pants. An idea popped into his mind. He poked the old man. 'Putting all that destiny stuff aside, we met some people on a world called Bewayre a few weeks ago. Their sun was dying. There wasn't much to eat. Horrible, cold place. Maybe that's why they smeared bogeys on each other. Perhaps it helped keep them warm.'

'So?' said Catsic.

'So, if this planet's empty, I think they'd be much

happier here,' said Alfie. 'They could stop eating each other and start eating fruit instead.'

'And *that*, right there, is you passing the test,' said Catsic, looking pleased. Getting to his feet he held out a hand. 'Maybe you're a little bit special after all, eh? Not many people would've thought of that, Alfie Fleet. The Bewayrian sun *is* dying. In three years it will go supernova, wiping out all life on Bewayre, and the planet itself. So you just saved millions of people, not to mention the lives of all their descendants who haven't been born yet. Rehoming the Bewayrians—or Clean Pantsians as I suppose they will become—will make a nice start to your new age of peace and exploration.'

'Yeah, I *really* need to come up with a better name for this planet,' said Alfie.

'Probably,' Catsic agreed. 'Still, well done. Not a bad morning's work for a funny little twonk with odd knees, eh? Now, let's go deal with Sir Willikin Nanbiter and claim your destiny, shall we? I will, of course, vote against him. He is an utter git, after all.'

Taking his hand, Alfie scrambled to his feet and

fished in his rucksack for *Lost Members of the Unusual Cartography Club*. 'Umm . . . I've been thinking about that . . .' he said.'

CHAPTER TWENTY-EIGHT

THE TABLES TURN

Planet Earth spun above the diamond circle.

'Would you look at that,' sighed Catsic the Henge, watching clouds swirling over the massive globe. '*Still* raining over Stonehenge. Some things never change, eh? Oh well, are we all ready?'

Derek shuffled to Alfie's side. 'Yup.'

'My father's going to thrash me to a *pulp*,' Flem groaned. 'Can I stay here? I *like* it here.'

'Easy,' said Catsic, clapping him on the shoulder. 'I have a feeling you'll be surprised.'

'I have a feeling I'm going to be carrying my bum around in a bag by the time he's finished with me,' Flem murmured.

'Bowell-Mouvemont reporting for duty,' said the Professor, saluting.

'Ready.' Alfie gulped, his heart racing. Like Flem, he wasn't much looking forward to seeing Sir Willikin again.

'We're ready, too,' said Pance.

'No one cares, you ghastly little parasite,' snapped Catsic. 'The rest of you, let's go change the universe, shall we?'

Once again, Alfie walked beneath a giant, diamond arch.

A second later he was home, stepping out into the dark cavern beneath Number Four, Wigless Square.

He grinned. Whatever happened next, at least he was on the same planet as his mum again. After the brightness of the diamond circle room his eyes took a few seconds to adjust to the gloom. The vast cavern was lit by a single candle. Sitting at a table, a few feet away, the Nanbiters glared at him.

'Hullo again,' Alfie said. 'Miss us?'

The only reply was a snarl from Sir Willikin.

Alfie's companions stepped out from the circle to stand beside him.

Sir Willikin shifted in his seat. The air seemed to darken around him. A dribble of pus trickled from his boil. Steepling his fingers, he growled, 'Well, well, well. Bowell-Mouvemont, Alfie Fleet, the Outlandish girl, Flemming . . . and this drooling beardy-weirdy must be Catsic the Henge, I suppose. So they found you, did they?'

'Pleased to meet you too,' said Catsic, peering around. '*Hate* what you've done with the place. Gloomy. Miserable. Smelly. Much like yourself.'

'SIIIII-LENCE,' roared Nanbiter, smashing a fist on the table. 'I am the President here and I demand respect . . .'

'Oh shut *up*,' Alfie interrupted, feeling his own anger rising. Only a couple of days had passed on Earth since he and his friends had left but Nanbiter obviously hadn't used the time to sit quietly and think about his behaviour. If anything it looked like something had come completely loose inside his already wonky brain.

Sir Willikin rose from his chair and leaned across the table. 'YOU!' he roared. 'I'll break every bone in your . . .'

Derek placed herself between them, her knife suddenly in her hand. 'Come one centimetre closer and you'll be wearing your lower intestine as a scarf,' she said, quietly.

'T'shup lesp, wing-a-schputt fruitcake, Derek,' Alfie muttered in Outlandish, from the corner of his mouth.

'Do I want to see your collection of dried kittens?'

Alfie winced. 'I meant, I'm glad destiny chose *you* to be my protector.'

'It's a rubbish job, but somone's got to do it,' Derek replied with a shrug.

'You're sort of like the Chosen One's Chosen One, really. If you stop and think about it.'

'Don't push your luck, twonk.'

'Willikin! *Willikin!* Do something,' squealed Lady Nanbiter. 'These *dreadful* people are *threatening* us.'

'Stiltskin,' Nanbiter bellowed. 'Pance. Get them! Get them NOW!'

'Sorry, Sir W,' said Pance, lifting his hands to show Nanbiter the ropes binding his wrists. 'Love to help but we're a bit tied up at the moment.'

Nanbiter turned a fierce shade of purple.

'Let's get this over with, shall we?' Alfie interruped. 'Sir Willikin, Pance tells me you know what we've been doing and why we're back, so please try to relax while we vote you out of the UCC.'

Slowly, Sir Willikin sat down. A vicious grin spread across his face. He looked at the Professor. 'Yes, let's get on with it,' he said, his tone suspiciously even. 'Before we begin, this shall be the final vote on who will be President of the Unusual Cartography Club, yes, Bowell-Mouvemont? You will never again seek to change the result, hmm? Agreed?'

'Agreed,' said the Professor. Putting his hand in the air, he went on, 'As President of the Unusual Cartography Club, now to be known as the Unusual Travel Agency, I vote for . . . Rupert . . . ahh, sorry Rupert, I seem to have forgotten your last name.'

Alfie gasped. 'What?'

'Oh yes: Rupert Watt. Silly of me.'

'No. I mean . . . *no*. You . . . you can't *do* that

Professor,' he yelped. '*You're* President.'

'Times change, eh?' the Professor answered, choking on his words a little. 'Old duffer now. Fresh leadership for a brighter tomorrow. Well deserved probation . . . proboscis . . . *promotion*. Congratulations, Rupert.'

'Alfie,' said Alfie, knowing it was hopeless. 'Alfie Fleet.'

'Of course, of course, of course. Sorry Rupert. Well done.'

'I vote for Rupert . . . I mean *Alfie*, too,' said Derek, raising her hand.

Alfie looked from his best friend to the Professor, tears springing to his eyes. 'You *guys*,' he murmured. Aloud, he said, 'I . . . well . . . I guess I do as well then. I vote for me. That's three votes, right?'

'It's *none*,' said Sir Willikin, leaning back in his chair and giggling. 'Oh dear, oh dear. Foolish old Sir Willikin. I forgot to mention that since you all left Number Four, Wigless Square against my orders, I expelled you from the Unusual Cartography Club. You are no longer members. None of you has the right to vote. Ooops.'

The Professor gasped. 'I say. That's hardly fa—'

'Still, let's continue shall we,' said Catsic. 'I, Catsic the Henge, vote for Alfie. Though, to be honest, I'd have voted for a small bag of chopped earwigs rather than you, Nanbiter.'

Sir Willikin's eyes narrowed. If looks could kill, his would have nailed the old man to the wall and played with his insides. 'So, Alfie Fleet has one vote,' he hissed. 'Pathetic. Let's finish this. I vote for myself, Sir Willikin Nanbiter.'

'And I,' sniffed his wife. 'My husband has my vote.'

'With Flemming, Pance, and Stiltskin, that makes five,' said Sir Willikin, triumphantly. 'You have failed, Alfie Fleet.'

'Umm,' said Flem in a tiny, squeaky voice.

He raised his hand. 'Alfie Fleet,' Nanbiter's son continued, just louder than the audible shaking of his knees. 'I vote for Alfie Fleet.'

'Thanks,' Alfie whispered, shooting him a sideways glance. 'Just for the record, I am really properly starting to like you.'

'Same,' squeaked Flem.

'*Flemming!*' squealed Lady Nanbiter. 'How *dare* you vote against your own father, and with these low-born gutterwallops, too!'

Nanbiter was on his feet again now, and shouting, 'Foul pustulence. I shall thrash your traitorous bottom. I shall thrash it until it comes OFF. You ... you ... beastly, spittle-faced ...' he stopped, staring at Pance, who had coughed. 'WHAT?' he roared.

'We're still members of the UCC, ain't we?' said Pance.

'Yes, yes, of course,' grunted Sir Willikin. 'Even though I have been stabbed in the back by my own flesh and blood I can still count on the votes of my faithful servants.'

'Nah,' said Stiltskin. 'Vote fer whatsisface.'

Sir Willikin's face, which had been displaying an impressive range of colours, now turned white. 'What?' he yelped.

'Me and Bernard vote for the boy,' said Pance. 'You deaf or something?'

'Eh?' Alfie gurgled, blinking at Pance and Stiltskin.

'You, too, betray us, Pance?' hissed Lady Nanbiter. 'After everything Sir Willikin's done for you?'

'Well yes,' said Pance, slowly, 'We *are* rogues, after all, and what Sir Willikin's done for us is lead us around a reee-*volting* planet no one wanted a map of in the first place. For *sixteen* years. Sixteen *miserable* years listening to that twazzock shouting orders at us. I'd be sick to the back teeth of it, if I had any back teeth. Plus, the boy's a worm-dangling sparrow-fart but he's got a destiny. I ain't getting in the way of that. Step too far, even for us. Isn't that right, Bernard, my sweet?'

'Yup,' said Stiltskin, nodding. 'Thass right.'

'I . . . uh . . . thanks, I suppose,' said Alfie.

'Don't go getting all squishy on us,' Pance replied. 'We're still black-hearted, vicious scum and proud of it, too.'

'You'll regret this. *All* of you,' Sir Willikin hissed.

'No we won't,' said Flem, his voice steadier. 'Even if we don't count the Professor, Alfie, or Derek it's four votes to two. We won. It's over, father. No one wanted you at the UCC five hundred years ago, and no one wants you here *now*. The Unusual Travel Agency must open. So *we* must leave.'

'No,' cackled Sir Willikin, scratching his boil. 'I don't think we *must*. Lights!' he shouted.

Instantly, the expensive spotlights of Number Four, Wigless Square's circle cavern flooded the room with blinding light.

'Count again, Alfie Fleet,' Sir Willikin crowed.

'You *didn't*,' croaked the Professor, looking around.

'I told the boy he'd have to get up early to get the better of me,' giggled Sir Willikin Nanbiter. 'Best not to go to bed at all.'

Alfie said nothing while he stared around at the people standing against the walls of the circle room. The Wigless Square postman was there. And the lady who ran the corner shop. There were a couple of bewildered homeless people who slept on a bench in Wigless Square's central garden, and more he didn't recognize.

'I made all these people *official* apprentices of the UCC while you were away,' sniggered Sir Willikin.

'According to the rules. I am *President*, after all. Shall we find out who they're going to vote for?'

'Err . . . we vote for Nanbiter,' mumbled one of the UCC's new members. 'Did we do that right? Can we go now? You're all very weird.'

'You have to put your hands up,' growled Nanbiter. 'Or you don't get paid.'

Forty-five hands were slowly raised.

'Nanbiter,' said forty-five voices. A person at the back added, 'Can I have my fifty pounds now?'

'Go,' sniffed Sir Willikin, as the last hand was raised. 'Get lost, the lot of you. Don't come back.' A stream of dribble drooled from the corner of his mouth. His boil erupted again as he turned back to Alfie. 'So, by forty-seven votes to four, I declare myself *still* the President of the Unusual Cartography Club. And as agreed, this shall be the final vote. Once again, you LOSE, Alfie Fleet. Now it's PUNISHMENT TIME!'

CHAPTER TWENTY-NINE

HOMECOMING

'But not all the votes have been counted,' said Alfie quietly.

'What fresh plotthrobbery is this?' Nanbiter roared. 'Have you lost your bipsy, boy? There's no one else here and . . .'

'Catsic, would you mind?' Alfie interrupted.

'My pleasure.' In a swirl of robes and beard, Catsic disappeared between the stones.

'The voting is OVER!' Nanbiter snarled.

Alfie shook his head, smiling. 'Silly man. The voting's not over,' he chuckled. 'Not by a long way. You were clever, Sir Willikin. I'll give you that. It was a fiendish idea, joining up new members of the UCC. You forgot something though.'

'What?' hissed Nanbiter, yellow goo dribbling down his face. 'What did I forget, you filthy little mump-bunty?'

'You forgot that I've *met* you,' said Alfie. 'And I know *exactly* what kind of person you are. So I asked myself, what would *I* do if I was Sir Willikin Nanbiter? What would *I* do if I was a complete and utter *git?*'

Any moment now, Alfie told himself, Sir Willikin was going to turn himself inside out with anger.

'Willikin! Are you just going to stand there and let this . . . this . . . absolute *specimen* insult you?' shrieked his wife.

'No. No I am NOT. Hand me my stick. I'm going to . . .'

Alfie held up a finger. 'Please let me finish,' he said. 'As I was saying, I *knew* you'd break all your own rules to hang on to power. A *secret* society only the worthy and fabulous could join, wasn't it? What rubbish.' Alfie shook his head, tutting before pulling *Lost Members of the Unusual Cartography Club* from his rucksack. 'Catsic has built the most *amazing* circle, Sir Willikin. Really. You wouldn't believe it. All kinds of extra features: automatic planet detection, surface scanner with zoom technology, a very handy cup-holder. He may look like a bearded raisin but he's *very* clever . . .'

Alfie paused, enjoying the changing colours of Sir Willikin's face: from white to red to purple mottled with green and then back to white. The noises coming from his mouth were entertaining, too. They were the sort of noises someone might make if forced to eat their own foot. Eventually, he went on, waving the book under Sir Willikin's nose. 'Time moves very slowly on Solstice, and we weren't in any hurry to get back,' he said. 'So we spent a few days visiting different planets. We found a lot more people than just Catsic the Henge, Sir Willikin. *Real* members of the UCC. They should be arriving about . . .'

The circle hummed.

'Oh hullo,' said a man with the exhausted face of a father-of-six and white curly hair, walking through the stones. He looked around the cavern.

'Been a while since I was here. Bit of a mess isn't it? Is that *donkey* poo on the carpet? You'll never get it out, you know.'

'*Jammy!*' squealed the Professor. 'Jammy Snuffgarden. I didn't know young Rupert had found *you*. How's the family?'

'*Pewsley*,' said Jammy Snuffgarden, taking his old friend's hand and pumping it up and down. 'It's been *ages*. Busy busy busy. But all's well. Spigott sends her love. So do Spigott, Spigott, Spigott, Spigott, and Spigott.'

'You can catch up in a minute Professor,' said Alfie. 'Mr Snuffgarden . . .'

'Oh yes.' Jammy Snuffgarden put his hand in the air. 'James Snuffgarden, Secretary of the Unusual Cartography Club from 1903 to 1928. I vote for anyone who isn't Sir Willikin Nanbiter as President.'

'That's one,' said Alfie, glancing at Sir Willikin and raising an eyebrow. 'Shall we carry on?'

Nanbiter made choking noises.

'Let's carry on,' said Alfie.

The stone circle hummed again.

'Emily Fuffkin, President of the Unusual

Cartography Club from 1546 to 1587, when I got lost on Hairpin V,' said an old woman, stepping out from between the stones. She was wearing a similar dress to Lady Nanbiter's except hers was cleaner and covered in pockets containing telescopes and map-making equipment. She looked Sir Willikin up and down. 'Still a great big molly hat, Willikin?' she sighed. 'You always were. Obviously, you cannot be allowed to control the UCC again so I vote for Alfie Fleet.'

'Thank you, Ms Fuffkin,' said Alfie.

Once more the circle hummed. 'Millard Hedge, UCC treasurer from 1497 to 1513,' said a large man with red cheeks, beaming around. 'Nice to be back. Oh . . . ah . . . Alfie Fleet, isn't it?' he finished, raising his hand.

The circle hummed again.

More lost-and-found members of the Unusual Cartography Club poured from between the stones. The circle room was filling fast with people wearing costumes stretching back centuries: men in tights and doublets, women with 1960s flower power hair-dos, and tall-hatted Victorians with moustaches to rival the Professor's.

The circle hummed and hummed again.

'Dimples McGee, Chief Cartographer and Librarian from 1926 to 1932. I vote for Alfie Fleet.'

'It's Alfie Fleet for me,' called another new arrival.

'Cedric Strangely-Brown, voting for Alfie Fleet.'

'I vote for Alfie Fleet.'

'Jeremy Ravenspoke,' called a man in a long wig, raising his hand. 'I vote for Sir Willikin Nanbiter ... just kidding. Alfie Fleet.'

And still they came.

'Enid Groviller, not quite as dead as everyone thought. Has anyone seen my trousers ... Oh, and I vote for Alfie Fleet.'

'Marcus Dominatus, Praesidem de singulari societatem chartus, XXIV ut XXXVII,' said a man wearing a toga. 'Ego te suffragium, Alfie Fleet.'

'Say again,' said Alfie, winding his translator.

'Marcus Dominatus, President of the Unusual Cartography Club from the years 24 to 37,' the Roman repeated. 'Voting for Alfie Fleet.'

'I make that sixty-eight votes for me, Sir

Willikin,' Alfie eventually called out over the babble of the crowd. The circle cavern was almost full now, the only space an empty circle around the Nanbiters.

Flem had been right.

Every time Alfie's name was shouted Sir Willikin Nanbiter's shoulders had sagged further. Lady Nanbiter dabbed at her eyes with a filthy hanky, while her husband stared at his feet, trembling. 'But . . . but it's not fair,' he moaned to himself. 'He's a boy. Just an apprentice. I'm Sir Willikin *Nanbiter*. The greatest President the UCC ever had . . .'

But the fight had gone out of him.

He had lost, and not even his own son had supported him.

Sir Willikin looked crushed.

'That's all of them,' said a loud voice.

Silence spread across the room. Catsic the Henge walked out from between the stones, pushing a waterlogged moped. Seaweed dripped from his beard.

'Betsy,' shrieked the Professor. 'Betsy Betsy Betsy.'

'Take it, boy,' grumped the old man, shoving the old moped at the Professor. 'And try not to lose it again. It's not my job to keep track of your things.'

Catsic paused, looking around over the heads of the assembled members of the UCC. 'Sir Willikin Nanbiter,' he said. 'It's time you were leaving.'

'But where shall we go?' yelped Lady Nanbiter, bursting into tears. 'Don't send us back to Bewayre. It was horrible. *Horrible.*'

'It's all you deserve,' said Catsic. 'But no. Solstice. There's a nice empty island where I'll be able to keep an eye on you. Also, I'll be needing your son.'

'Eh?' said Flem, looking up.

'I'm an old man,' Catsic continued. 'Frankly, the only reason I'm not dead yet is because I play cards with Death, and I *cheat*. But you can't cheat Death forever and one day soon I shall build the Dark Circle that will take me on my final adventure. Long story short: I need an apprentice, Flemming Nanbiter, and destiny has fingered *you* for the job. You'll be in charge of finding planets, working with the Unusual Travel Agency to change the future of the universe.'

'I'll be in charge of the diamond circle?' said Flem, his eyes shining. 'And all those books, too? *Cool*. Very well, I accept. I *shall* be your apprentice.'

'Yes, I *know*, you little twerp,' said Catsic, giving Flem a soft cuff round the back of the head. 'What part of the word "destiny" don't you understand?'

CHAPTER THIRTY

THE UTA'S GRAND OPENING

Three days later, the stone circle cavern beneath Number Four, Wigless Square was stuffed with people holding plates and wondering how they were supposed to eat with a glass in the other hand. Old friends from Book One were there, as well as travel writers and journalists. Captain Swag, dressed in rags and freshly rescued from a desert island, told pirate jokes to the UCC members who'd stuck around to see the UTA's official opening. The dragon diamond Alfie's mum had sold had paid a lot of decorators to work fast and the place was looking spiffy again. New metal letters hung on the wall.

Gleaming beneath expensive spotlights, they spelled out THE UNUSUAL TRAVEL AGENCY. Stacks of freshly printed brochures were piled on the shiny gift shop counter. New stock—including mugs and t-shirts—sat on polished shelves. The carpet was new, too. Fairy lights hung from the ceiling, and smartly-dressed waiters wandered through the crowd carrying trays of cheese puffs and miniature prawn sandwiches.

Prince Hoodwink, sipping from a glass crammed with fruit and umbrellas through a long straw, looked at Alfie over the top of his ridiculously large sunglasses and said, 'So, I hear you're the Chosen One now.'

The elven prince was wearing skintight silver trousers and a white fur coat with a bobble hat over his pointy ears. While anyone else would have looked a total pranny, Alfie had to admit that Hoodwink looked *fabulous*. He was, after all, the world's leading male supermodel. 'Well, yeah,' Alfie said, blushing. 'It's—y'know—not really a proper job title but . . .'

Hoodwink wasn't listening. 'Hey, Sparklelegs,'

he shouted across the cavern room to another elf who was almost—but not quite—as good-looking as the prince. 'He says he's the Chosen One.'

'Who?' shouted back another elf. He was wearing traditional elf gear of tunic and boots with a bow over his shoulder and his gorgeously shiny copper hair held back with a golden circlet.

'Alfie Fleet,' yelled Hoodwink. 'You know— the human we hunted in Hinderwood. The ugly one. This is his party. Anyway, he reckons he's the Chosen One.'

Alfie cringed with embarrassment.

'Chosen One?' Sparklelegs snorted. 'Chosen for what? To rule over all the people with weird knees or something?'

'I don't know, I'll ask him,' Hoodwink called back. Turning back to Alfie, he asked, 'Chosen for what?'

Blushing, Alfie replied: 'It's my destiny to bring the universe into a new age of peace and harmony through intergalactic tourism.'

'What did he say?' Sparklelegs called over.

'Something about destiny,' shouted Hoodwink. 'I lost interest. *Bo*-ring.'

'Look,' said Alfie, changing the subject. 'Can you do a cover shoot, Hoodwink? I'm writing a new travel guide. I thought a photo of you, leaning against a stone circle or something.'

'Yes, yes, have your people talk to my people,' said Hoodwink, with a wave of a hand. 'Nice party, by the way. Terrible music though.'

'Sorry about that. Lord Poobin would only agree to do the food if we booked General Grome, too.' Alfie glanced into the corner where the goblin general was tinkling the keys of his piano and crooning his latest song, a jaunty number called *Blunt Force Trauma*. Lord Poobin had done a great job with the food though. Alfie snatched a dainty muffin from a passing tray.

'Oh there you are, sweetie,' said his mum, interrupting. 'Hullo Hoodwink, you big preening ninny. Mind if I borrow Alfie?'

'Not at all,' said Hoodwink, failing to hide a yawn. 'He's boring me to death. Blah blah, Chosen One. Blah blah, destiny. What about me? Why aren't we talking about *me?*'

'Come along, love. You should say something to all these people,' said Alfie's mum, taking him by the elbow and steering him through the crowd.

'Yeek.' Alfie stopped. 'Do I *have* to?'

'You've vanquished dragons and Nanbiters. It can't be any worse than that.'

'That's what you think,' Alfie told her, looking around at the crowd, nervously. The idea of standing on the circle platform and speaking to the whole room made him feel a bit weak in the bladder area. 'Thanks for all this, by the way, mum. For getting the place fixed up so fast. We'll pay you back. That is, the Unusual Travel Agency will pay you back.'

'It already has,' said his mum. 'I've been taking bookings all night. Trips to visit the Mystical Serpent of Nerwong Nerwong Plinky-Plonk are surprisingly popular, and Debbi Puddlebeak is going to be *very* busy. Winspan trips are selling like . . .' Spotting a flame-haired woman in sparkling armour, she continued, 'Oh, hello Sir Brenda. I wanted to talk to you about the first Outlandish quest, next week. It looks like you'll be leading a party of twelve into the Howling Palace of Endless Pain. Three families, two with children under six.'

Sir Brenda lifted a glass to her lips. 'I'll bring some of our Howling Pain kiddies' lunchboxes,' she murmured. 'Hello, Dragonslayer.'

'Sir Brenda,' Alfie bowed, winding his translator again. 'How's Verminium?'

'Fine, fine,' grinned the knight. 'The minstrels still sing of your adventures. My personal favourite is *Rupert, the Idiot Who Buried All the Gold Under a Mountain of Rubble*. I could sing it for you if you like. Very catchy . . .'

'Spin't toferr c-shang-a-lang limply soup, Sir Brenda,' said Alfie, spotting a chance to practise his Outlandish. The device around his neck picked up the words and spat them out: 'I'd rather you didn't, Sir Brenda.'

Alfie frowned. He gave the translator a shake, barely listening while Sir Brenda sang

His knees were weird and his heart was bold,
The idiot boy who destroyed the gold.

His name was Rupert!
Oh Rupert, you utter spanner . . .

'If you'll excuse me, Sir Brenda, there's a couple of people over there I should talk to,' said Alfie. He pushed through the crowd, leaving his mum tapping her foot.

'It *is* very catchy,' she told Sir Brenda before shouting after Alfie, 'Go and say something, son.'

Alfie pretended not to hear. Dodging through the crowd, he stopped in front of Incontinence Pance and Bernard Stiltskin. The two of them were huddled together, looking lonely. 'Oh, it's you two,' Alfie said, gruffly. 'I forgot you were still here. I suppose I'd better do something with you.'

'You ain't gonna throw us out, are you, you nasty little spink widdler?' said Pance, glaring through the one good lens of his spectacles. 'We ain't got nowhere else to go.'

Alfie ignored him, leading them up to a small group of people wearing black studded leather. 'This is Gerald Teethcrusher of Outlandish,' he said. 'Owner of the Thank Goodness it's Teethcrusher's chain of restaurants and leader of a band of villainous scum.'

Gerald Teethcrusher grinned and took a swig from the dirty tankard he was carrying. After an enormous burp, he said, 'Ahh, you cannot beat a pint of cat wee. Hullo, young dragonslayer. 'Ave you heard the new song? It's a big hit all across Outlandish. I'll sing it for you if you like. It goes . . .'

'I've heard it,' Alfie sighed. 'Gerald, I want you to meet Incontinence Pance and Bernard Stiltskin. They'd fit right into your gang of scoundrels, and probably make good waiters if you're looking for staff. Well, *terrible* waiters, really, but they'd suit the atmosphere at Thank Goodness it's Teethcrusher's.'

'Would you just look at this, fellas,' said one of the villainous scum, grabbing Pance by the hair. 'I've never seen anyone more in need of a hot oil treatment and a restyle. When did you last have this cut?'

'Err . . . about five hundred years ago,' said Pance. 'What's it gotta do with you?'

'Manly Todd is only *part-time* villainous scum,' Alfie explained. 'Most of the time he's a hairdresser.'

He left the little group chatting to Nanbiter's ex-henchmen, smiling to himself. He was already fulfilling his destiny. People from different ends of the universe were getting to know each other.

The Professor's voice floated across the room. Alfie made his way towards him. The old man was in full flow.

'So there I was, Jammy, trapped with my finger in a . . . oh, what do you call them? No don't tell me, I'll get it in a moment. Umm . . . panda. Yes. No. *Was* it a panda or was it a Dogbeardian finger-trap? Anyway, it was *fiendishly* difficult to get my finger out of this panda and Vlad Saladhater, the greasy king of Whoopsie! was slithering closer and closer. By this time, of course, my broken ankle was giving me *terrible* gyp . . . Oh, Rupert, there you are.'

'Professor, Mr Snuffgarden,' said Alfie. 'I hope you're enjoying the party.'

'Oh yes, lovely . . . Ahh, I think you're wanted, Rupert,' said the Professor, waving his drink towards the circle platform where Catsic was tapping his foot, impatiently. Flem stood at his side, whispering something in Derek's ear. She laughed.

Leaving the Professor happily twittering on to the Spigotts, Alfie made his way over. 'Hi Catsic,' he said. 'How are the Clean Pantsians settling in on their new planet?'

'I'm afraid they've renamed it SnotSnotSnotSnot,' said Catsic. 'It might take them a while to lose their old ways. No one's eaten each other yet, though.'

'And Flem, I'll be seeing you soon, I guess?'

Flem nodded. 'I'll bring you files on some new worlds to look at in a day or two,' he said.

'Thanks. And how are your mum and dad?'

'Father's renamed their little island the Empire of Sir Willikin,' Flem sighed. 'He's building an army of crabs. I think we broke him a bit too much, but he seems happy enough.'

'Say hi for me when you next see him.'

'No, I don't think I'll do that. He starts punching himself in the face whenever your name is mentioned.'

Turning to Derek, Alfie said, in Outlandish, 'Whiffly ch-spank spank hroo dumpling, Derek?'

'You want a rotating butt handle?' said Derek. '*Really?*'

Alfie wound the handle on his translator again. "Whiffly ch-spank spank hroo dumpling, Derek,' he repeated. The translator translated the words 'How's it going, Derek?' coming from its tiny trumpet.

Alfie stared at Derek, raising an eyebrow. 'Fam fam, Derek. Cherrrt t'popsy spindly t'spip pesto,' he said.

'Well, well, Derek' the translator said. 'Apparently I speak Outlandish just fine.'

'*Busted,*' said Derek, with a shrug. 'Saving your life gets dull. A girl's got to keep herself entertained.'

'Destiny chose you to look out for me, not . . .' said Alfie.

'I never signed anything,' Derek butted in.

'Yeah but, I'm fairly sure destiny didn't mean for you to . . .'

'If you've finished squabbling, Flemming and I are leaving,' Catsic interrupted, flipping his beard over a shoulder. 'I'm taking the rest of the old UCC members back where they came from. Most of them at least.'

'Thank you for all your help,' Alfie said, shaking the old man's hand. 'Couldn't have done it without you.'

'I know,' said Catsic. 'So, if you were going to say a few words . . .'

Alfie blushed. 'Do I *have* to?' he muttered.

'No one said being the Chosen One would be easy,' Catsic told him.

'But . . .'

'Just get on with it, you weird-kneed little twit.'

Turning to face the room, Alfie coughed.

General Grome stopped playing.

Silence spread.

Alfie looked across the sea of faces, all staring at him. 'S-So,' he squeaked. 'I just wanted to say . . .'

'Speak up, dearie,' yelled a voice. 'I can't hear a word he's saying. Can you, Mavis?'

'Turn on your ear trumpet, you daft trout. Carry on young man. Don't mind Dot.'

A smile spread across Alfie's face. 'Ladies and gentlemen,' he said, his voice sounding more confident. 'Witches, wizards, goblins, dark lords, noble heroes, elves, villainous scum, intrepid holidaymakers, and assorted weirdoes from other planets. Welcome to the Unusual Travel Agency. Tonight, the universe is open for business. Book early to avoid disappointment. And don't forget to visit our gift shop.'

ALFIE FLEET'S GUIDE to the UNIVERSE

INTRODUCTION

If you're interested in the universe, or
ANYTHING in it, this is the book for
you! For the first time in thousands of
years travellers can now use Stone Circle™
technology to explore the whole of space
once again. Thousands of planets are waiting
to welcome **YOU** today.

Packed with detailed guides to more than
fifty worlds, featuring maps, great sightseeing
opportunities, and guest reviews from fellow
universe-hoppers, *Alfie Fleet's Guide to
the Universe* will help you find your best
INTERGALACTIC holiday.

ImboHagredge Phembly country

KEGNOGG Water Transport

NEEDLEHEAD SECONDARY SCHOOL

MADAME GERALD BLAIR'S House

Stepping stone bridge

THE UPSIDE DOWN MUSEUM

NUMBLETONNES CITY

border into New Seal Land

DEAD MAN'S LAND

MOUNT ZERO

WISHBONE WOOD

DEATHPRISM VALLEY

Slidysnake Path

Mount Zero's Flyfish Lake

SKULL DESERT

eNN C Hammton's Windmill Peake rhubarb meadows

Eggie primp Clocktower

WEDGE-O-CHEEZ PALACE

The Delbo Hole

Orbiting the small star of Terro Cherro is the world of **Shrimpest**, where travellers will find the exciting nation of **Imbohagredge**. This is one of the universe's chillier planets, so don't forget to pack warm underwear! Popular with travellers who like rhubarb, warm mittens, and rhubarb, **Imbohagredge** scores highly on the Fleet Unusuality Scale and is a great destination for anyone who likes to be thoroughly freaked out while eating rhubarb. Those braving the -0.03 degree temperatures will find a world brimming with unusual architecture, including the spectacular Wedge-o-Cheez Palace, which has been voted "Most Bonkers Palace or Castle in the Universe" ten times running. Madame Geraldi Blair's House—designed to look like an octopus's head—the Upsicle-Down Museum, the Eggieprimp Clocktower, Numbletonnes City, and Needlehead Secondary School are also well worth a visit for fans of really, really, really odd buildings.

Imbohagredge has much more to offer though, especially for rhubarb lovers. Here you'll find endless meadows of the stuff. If you don't like rhubarb, don't worry—you'll soon learn to love it. As any Imbohagredgian will tell you: you either love rhubarb or starve to death.

DEATHPRISM VALLEY

Visit Deathprism Valley for amazing views of this hundreds-of-mile-long prism. The only object on Imbohagredge that can be seen from Shrimpest's eighteen neighbouring galaxies, the locals are extremely proud of their massive prism. Everyone else thinks they're freaks.

THE DELBO HOLE

As they say on **Imbohagredge**, 'If you like holes, you'll LOVE the Delbo Hole.' And they're right. Wherever else you go in the universe you won't find a hole that's holier than the Delbo Hole. Don't forget to book in advance. As you might expect, the Delbo Hole is an extremely busy tourist attraction.

DISCOVERING . . . PLANET BALDY

A Stage Seven planet on the UCC's Haircut Guide to Civilization Development, visitors to **Planet Baldy** will enjoy the exquisite views of sunshine reflecting on bald heads, and the atmosphere of peaceful tranquillity of this serene garden planet. The locals banging tambourines and chanting can get a little bit annoying though. Tourists exploring this deeply mystical world, dotted with pyramids and restaurants serving explosively spicy dishes should check out some of the planet's attractions . . .

Yoga on Baldy

Learn the famous Stuttering Ferret position and put both feet up your own nostrils on a yoga retreat with Guru Wobbli Rubbahlegs Bindibendi!

The Pyramid of Didyoustealmycoatzl

The planet's most magnificent pyramid rises nearly 2,000 feet into the clouds. Dedicated to the god of Supreme-Oneness-With-All-Things, locals wearing only sacred swimming costumes make the long and difficult climb to the summit at dawn each day. Here they solemnly meditate beneath the golden mask of Didyoustealmycoatzl before whizzing down the amazing water slides to the Reflecting Pool of Serenity at the base of the pyramid.

THE OBSERVATORY OF MAGI

Planet Baldy is famous for its end-of-the-universe predictions, which are based on scientific study of the stars and planets by the city's magi. Of course, scientists find it difficult to agree on anything and some say the entire universe will be destroyed 2,000 years in the future, during the Year of the Still-Throbbing-Llama. Others insist it ended last Tuesday. Climb to the top of the observatory for excellent views, though—due to a design fault—it's impossible to see any actual stars or planets.

WHERE TO STAY

The Royal Hotel *

Walking through the solid gold doors into the plush surroundings of the Royal Hotel, where scented fountains tinkle and soft candlelight plays off exquisite furniture, you might think you're in real royal palace. You are. And you'll instantly be chased out by the guards. The hotel is a mosquito-infested shack round the back.

WHERE TO STAY

Stacko Tacko ✱✱✱

Popular with the locals, Stacko Tacko dares
customers to try its Volcano Hot Quadruple
Chilli Tacko—a dish so spicy it melts the eyeballs
of anyone stupid enough to try it. Those brave
enough to take the challenge can win a Stacko
Tacko T-shirt and their name on the Wall of
Flame.

DISCOVERING . . . THE ENDLESS EMPIRE

Just the name of **the Endless Empire**
conjures picturesque images of vast, sweeping
landscapes and thousands of years of fascinating
tradition. Sadly, it has been badly misnamed.
The Endless Empire was founded
last year in a small valley on **Planet
Schminglestein** and measures about three
miles long by twenty feet wide. It has been
ruled by the ninety-eight-year-old Everlasting
Emperor for only three weeks. Sadly, he is not

expected to everlast much longer as parts of him (one leg, his left ear) are already dead.

WHERE TO STAY

Taverna Goatolovina ***

The only place to eat in the Endless Empire is the Endless Empire's only restaurant. Here, visitors dine by torchlight, surrounded by wasp nests, while host, 'Big Mikos', smashes plates, glasses, and customers' heads during his famous Grunting Belly Dance. On the plus side, this scares away most of the wasps.

NEW AT THE
UTA GIFT SHOP

General Grome's incredible new album, 'Throat Squeezer', available now only from the Unusual Travel Agency gift shop. Contains the chart-breaking singles *Agonizing Pain Crumpet*, *Gnome is Where the Heart is*, *Scorpion Trousers*, and the heartbreaking new ballad *Flies, Flies, Flies on a Corpse*.

'Like being strangled with your own intestines. Brilliant!'
***** *Jamie Fringe*

XARDOX:
A PLANET, NOT
A TOILET ROLL.

I ♥
3,000
FARTS

Keep it **FRIMPY,** Frimpdude

THE UNUSUAL TRAVEL AGENCY:

LONDON, NEW YORK, STONEHENGE

CAPTAINS SWAG'S
LUXURY CRUISES

All aboard the
JEWEL OF THE BREEZY SEAS II
for the luxury cruise
of a lifetime

Ugly People

THE *sensational* NEW
FRAGRANCE BY PRINCE HOODWINK.
FOR MEN, FOR WOMEN*

** Causes persistent itchy rashes
when used by men, or women.
Spraying on any part of the body
not recommended. Keep away from
children, pets, and houseplants.*

ACKNOWLEDGEMENTS

My thanks to all the fabulous staff at Oxford University Press and especially Kathy Webb and Debbie Sims, who remained very relaxed while a couple of deadlines zipped past, as well as for keeping me on the straight and narrow. A big shout out, too, to Rob Lowe: designer extraordinaire. Alfie Fleet's adventures are brought to life by the amazing talents of Mr Chris Mould and for that I remain truly grateful. If you haven't got hold of a copy of his Iron Man book, you really should. My spectacular agent, Penny Holroyde, also gets massive props for being such a class act. Mostly though, thanks to my amazing family and particularly my mum and dad, Annette and Colin. Without their constant support over decades none of this would have been possible. I love you both.

Mart x

MARTIN HOWARD

Martin Howard is a raffle-winning author who took first prize (a girl's bike) at the Holtspur Middle School Summer Fete in 1986. Although he makes fun of fantasy and sci-fi books he is a massively nerdy fan of both, and likes a good laugh, too. Martin prefers to be called Mart, talks in his sleep, enjoys toast, and lives in France with his wife, three children, and a grumpy dog called Licky.

CHRIS MOULD

Chris is an award-winning illustrator who went to art school at 16. A sublime draughtsman with a penchant for the gothic, he has illustrated the gamut from picture books and young fiction, to theatre posters and satirical cartoons for national newspapers. He lives in Yorkshire with his wife, has two grown-up daughters, and when he's not drawing and writing, you'll find him... actually, he's never not drawing or writing.

Ready for more incredible adventures? Try these!

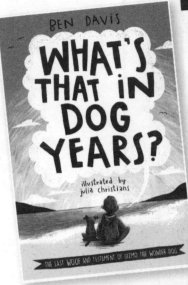

BEN DAVIS

WHAT'S THAT IN DOG YEARS?

illustrated by julia christians

THE LAST WOOF AND TESTAMENT OF GIZMO THE WONDER DOG

A DOUBLE DETECTIVES MEDICAL MYSTERY

THE CURE FOR A CRIME

ROOPA FAROOKI

TOM McLaughlin

ATTACK OF THE SMART SPEAKERS

EIGHT-LEGGED AND POWER-HUNGRY

ELAINE WICKSON — she wrote it

CHRIS JUDGE — he did the pictures

PLANET STAN

MY LIFE IN PIE CHARTS

Random mates

Level 5 humiliation

Snail carnage

Utter brother chaos

Beetroot cake of doom

A NORMAL LIFE!!!